LULLABIES & ALIBIS

Lullabies & Alibis

A NOVEL

STEPHANIE D. LEWIS

COPYRIGHT © 2008 BY STEPHANIE D. LEWIS.

LIBRARY OF CONGRESS CONTROL NUMBER: 2008901829
ISBN: HARDCOVER   978-1-4363-2586-8
             SOFTCOVER   978-1-4363-2585-1

All rights reserved. No part of this book may be reproduced or transmitted in any form or by any means, electronic or mechanical, including photocopying, recording, or by any information storage and retrieval system, without permission in writing from the copyright owner.

This is a work of fiction. Names, characters, places and incidents either are the product of the author's imagination or are used fictitiously, and any resemblance to any actual persons, living or dead, events, or locales is entirely coincidental.

This book was printed in the United States of America.

To order additional copies of this book, contact:
Xlibris Corporation
1-888-795-4274
www.Xlibris.com
Orders@Xlibris.com
47391

DEDICATIONS

For my father, Joseph Mark, (Moe Jark) for believing.

For my husband, Ron, for supporting and loving.

For my mother, Adrienne, for affirming the sunshine.

For my brother, Randall, for the laughter.

For my grandmother, Ethel Mark, for embracing life.

For my Aunt, Carol Mark, for proofing with a sense of humor. And for purses.

For my Uncle, Gary Mark, for treating me like an adult.

For Mitchell, Benjamin, Dustin, Jamisyn, Eliza & Desmond for simply being.

For all those who endured a little "Nordis Spect" throughout the years.

CONTENTS

Acknowledgments 9
Prologue: Listen Up! 11
Chapter 1:   Fully Clothed and Fully Disclosed 15
Chapter 2:   Sonogram Has the Word Son in It 19
Chapter 3:   Don't Look, Don't Touch 23
Chapter 4:   One Thing Leads to Another 27
Chapter 5:   Sugar and Spice and 31
Chapter 6:   A Mother's Work is Never Undone 35
Chapter 7:   Making a Scene 41
Chapter 8:   Groggy and Foggy 43
Chapter 9:   It's Not "Weather" You Win or Lose 47
Chapter 10:   A Stitch in Time 51
Chapter 11:   The Breast Test 55
Chapter 12:   Baby Face 61
Chapter 13:   Zealous and Jealous 65
Chapter 14:   Pat That Hat 69
Chapter 15:   Colder and Bolder in Boulder 71
Chapter 16:   Wish You Were Here 77
Chapter 17:   Sight for Sore Eyes 81
Chapter 18:   Worth A Thousand Words 85
Chapter 19:   "Grate" Expectations 89
Chapter 20:   The Moment of Ruth 93
Chapter 21:   Seeing Red 99
Chapter 22:   Seal the Deal 103
Chapter 23:   Connecting the Dots 109
Chapter 24:   Dream Extreme 111
Chapter 25:   To Unhinge a Binge 115
Chapter 26:   The Prozac Prelude 119
Chapter 27:   The Naked Truth 123
Chapter 28:   "Scene" But Not Heard 129
Chapter 29:   Depth Perception 135
Chapter 30:   My World Wide Web 139

Chapter 31: When Skies Are Gray 147
Chapter 32: The Doctor Is In 151
Chapter 33: Optical "Allusions"..155
Chapter 34: Ruth's Story 159
Chapter 35: The Sam Exam 165
Chapter 36: Removed..169
Chapter 37: Such a Touch 175
Chapter 38: Past, Present, and Future Tense 179
Chapter 39: Predictions...185
Chapter 40: The Missing "Peace"..189
Chapter 41: Gutter Grown Gardenias...193
Chapter 42: Noises Off..197
Chapter 43: The Shallow End 201

Acknowledgments

In the physical making of this book, I wish to thank Dustin Atlas for his clever cover art (concept and design) as well as Mitchell Atlas for his technical skills in the physical implementation of the book cover. Immense gratitude is also extended to Carol Mark and Ron Lewis for their detail-oriented proofreading skills.

In the emotional journey of this book, I wish to express sincere appreciation to my first writing professor, Katharine Haake, a distinguished author and cherished instructor. It is under her expert teachings that the Nordis Spect Tales first materialized in short story form in 1987. I am so grateful for the strong females who have offered support in the form of an ear, shoulder or pom-pom, including Helene, Cyra, Emma, Lorraine, Brenda, Devra, Rebecca, Violet, Elsa, Donna, Deb, Randi, Sheri, Gail, Deborah, Valerie, and Susan.

A tremendous thank-you for all the nameless women on the "Gender Disappointment" boards who poured their hearts out to me as well. May they always find comfort and empathy. Speaking of comfort, I'm forever indebted to Dr. Paul Fox, a brilliant doctor who *clearly* renewed my life in 1981. My children have been extraordinarily patient and not only do they have my thanks, they have extra treats coming their way!

Lastly, endless love goes out to Ron who, while rivaling the best comedians, has been painstakingly tolerant throughout the entire process only to gallantly take on more than he probably ever could've conceived. You'll always be my favorite genre.

Prologue

LISTEN UP!

I'm an eavesdropper. I've learned that listening in is a good way to read someone's mind if you're not psychic. You get to know exactly what they're thinking just as sure as if they had one of those thought bubbles over their heads with printed words, like they draw in comic strips. And believe me—eavesdropping is a necessary skill for survival in a world populated mainly by actors and actresses. The first time I overheard a conversation on the sly was quite by accident.

I was in the fourth grade with my two best friends, Jane and Kate. Famished well before the lunch bell, (I was always skipping breakfast to lose weight) I snuck in the utility closet where Mrs. Baker kept our belongings, to wolf down my sandwich. I heard approaching girlish chatter and realized Jane and Kate, who carpooled together, had arrived late and were coming inside to stow their stuff. I stopped mid-chew to hear their giggles and gab, crouching on a Partridge Family metal lunch box, well obscured by the coat rack.

"Let's not sit near Nordis in the cafeteria anymore," Kate said.

"Yeah, it's so embarrassing with her smelly lunch," Jane agreed. I sniffed my half-eaten tuna sandwich, crinkling my ten-year-old nose.

"You sit against the wall and I'll make sure Julie sits on my other side." Cattiness in the making.

"Okay, but tell Julie to make it seem like an accident," orchestrated Jane.

They scurried out when Mrs. Baker called the class to order for music, which was my favorite part of the day. That morning I skipped *My Country Tis of Thee* in favor of devouring the rest of the goodies my mother packed me.

After that, I nauseously went to the nurse with enough remarkable symptoms to warrant a call home, which of course resulted in a pick-up by my father just before that dreaded lunch hour.

A few years later, the next eavesdropping scenario would find me outside my parents' bedroom, ear pressed to their door after detecting an argument brewing between them that had been quashed at dinner. This was obvious because my mother had calmly said, "This isn't an appropriate place for a discussion like this, Max," and raised her brows at my father over the candlesticks. I just had to know what they were going to fight over. Turns out it was about me.

"It's definitely time for that girl to get a bra, Max."

Maybe I'll be getting one, but I won't be wearing one, I thought.

"Leave it alone Judith, she's got plenty of time to be a woman. Will you let her be a little girl?"

Thanks Dad, I thought and glanced at my burgeoning chest.

"Okay, if you don't mind the gardener stroking his hose and salivating by your little girl's bedroom window. Because that's what I observed today." I considered this—ew.

"I'll tell you," she continued, "it's not proper, her gallivanting around carefree as if she's got a normal body. She's also gotten a bit chunky around her upper arms."

"Don't they do that before their growth spurt?"

"Maybe so, but I'm not taking any chances."

That night she served dry salmon and broccoli and announced our entire family was adopting healthier eating habits.

Two days later, the next situation occurred during seventh grade P.E. class. Showers were mandatory, which was laughable since nobody broke a sweat tapping croquet balls. Nevertheless, a naked roll-call had to be endured with just two feet of white terrycloth to cover your body. Sometimes Miss Brody even peeked under to check for water droplets present on your skin—proof of good hygiene. My next class was science and on this particular day, I climbed in my gym locker to see if the phosphorous paint on my solar system project still glowed in the dark. Two popular classmates walked by and I heard enough snatches of their conversation to know I was the subject again.

"She is such a slut, flaunting her tits are big enough for a bra."

"Um, I know. Acting all upset when the boys snap it in Algebra."

"Yeah, you know she just loves getting all that . . ." And they were gone.

From that day on, I hid in a bathroom stall with a towel wrapped around my overgrown, bare body—my feet propped up to prevent detection and my teeth clamped to keep from chattering. When the shrill whistle blew for shower check, I splashed water from the sink onto my shoulders and blended nonchalantly in line.

The most recent incident occurred when I was pregnant and exhausted from having my mother over for dinner. After bidding everyone goodnight, I retired upstairs early, then snuck back onto the landing to listen to my husband and mother play gin. In between hands, there were some fascinating offhand remarks.

"So she got another rejection slip today. They really do a number on her head," my husband remarked as he dealt cards.

"You want that six? Perhaps she just doesn't have the talent to get published," came from my mother.

"Well, you know. Talent or no talent, they say it's really hard to break in. If the editors would only write something encouraging next to the box checked 'No,' she wouldn't get so depressed."

"You know what, Nathan? Get to the mail first next time and write something flattering. Then tell her you opened it because you were excited. And because you support her writing career. Gin."

"You're such a card, Judith." One of Nathan's famous puns. "Your deal."

When I was sure they were done discussing me, I crept up to bed and reread the short story I had submitted. It was pure crap.

The next day, Nathan handed me a rejection letter with stilted handwriting in the margin. It said, "You've got incredible talent, just not right for us. Thanks!"

Chapter 1

FULLY CLOTHED AND FULLY DISCLOSED

> *"Oh what a tangled web we weave,*
> *When first we practice to deceive!"*
>
> Sir Walter Scott (1771-1832)
> and
> My Mother (Infinity)

Many people want me on medication. Some, like my mother, think antidepressants are the ticket to make me anti-miserable. But there are those, including my husband, who would opt for anti-anxiety drugs to de-agonize me. But none of these pill-popping enthusiasts realize just how resourceful I can be on my own, coping with the sheer liquidity of my negative emotions.

Emotions are like water, and I'm not a skilled swimmer—especially off the deep end. Those drips and dribbles of disappointment that trickle into daily existence, those potent squirts of panic that life sprays at you on dark evenings—those are fairly easy for me to mop up. It's the sudden, pipe-bursting gush of undiluted heartache that drowns me every time. But lately I think I'm onto a solution—a good, creative way to drain all the flash floods and get my life flowing normally once again.

But first let me say that keeping secrets is not the same thing as lying. I know a lot about both. Secrets are justifiably kept to protect people, including the secret-keeper herself. For instance, no one needs to know that I used to be overweight—especially my husband. If I move to a new city where nobody realizes what I looked like previously and destroy all my old photographs, then I have every right to begin life anew as a thin person. Don't I?

What I'm saying is there's not a dire need for inane phrases like "back when you were heavy and wore only black . . ." or "If you eat all that, you might be sorry," to be interjected into everyday conversations. And my mother should not feel she's a dishonest person if she refrains from regaling her dinner party friends with her tried and true crowd-pleaser, "How my daughter lost fifty pounds on the Atkin's diet" story. Agreed?

I mean it's not like she's a guest getting interviewed, and Oprah says, "Now tell our studio audience Judith, isn't it true that at one time your daughter weighed twice what she does now?" Should this ever be the case, I agree she'd be free to give any answer she prefers because you shouldn't hold back on Oprah. She can even offer up one of her silly quotations like, "A moment on the lips, forever on the hips."

You see, my mother pens a local newspaper column here in Los Angeles and she calls herself, "*The Quote Gal*," because each week a famous quotation leads off her article. With her personality, it wouldn't be outlandish if you guessed her to be a gossip columnist, but thankfully she's not. I guess my own love of language and writing must come from her. But my intensity definitely comes from my father. And a few other things.

My main point is it's completely inappropriate to have my fairly new husband worry that I might insidiously become a chubby wife, just because my mother likes to be the one to dispense interesting tidbits about people's pasts at cocktail parties. And it's not fair to have everyone I've just recently befriended inspecting my thighs, scrutinizing my stomach, essentially watching and weighting, (wow, that was quite the Freudian slip, wasn't it?) waiting for me to gain all my poundage back, (and then some) just because statistics (and they could be Oprah's statistics) say I will.

But my mother really crossed the line when she decided our new neighborhood should be made aware of the prior problems with my eldest boy. Some things should be allowed to stay in the past. That's just taking her "honesty is the best policy" concept too far. She spoiled future babysitting jobs for him and she could've ruined my engagement too. It's one thing to bring normal baggage to a second marriage, but I'm sure Nathan would've changed his mind completely if he knew he was marrying someone who toted a suitcase with a broken lock. We all deserve a second chance. So if someone tries to make a fresh start—don't scribble on their clean slate. You getting this, Mom?

To review then, secrets omit information but lying actually distorts reality to suit your own purposes. Like the time I was fourteen, we took a family vacation and I decided I hated my name. I mean really, what normal teenage girl would take any sort of pride in a name like this? The name Colette sounds charming, chic, charismatic, captivating and . . . French, (I ran out of C adjectives) that trust me; you'd be tempted to adopt it as your name too. Especially if you were approached on a Hawaiian beach by a young and studley surfer dude named Randy.

And after the name change, it's just a short sand's throw away to alter other details in your boring life. You're employed as a part-time hair model and you had to drop out of a national ice-skating competition because you twisted your ankle during rehearsal. No worries, it's all good. (I actually hate when people use that expression.) But really, you only innocuously flirted with someone for one week out of an entire summer during your teenage years. And you knew your paths would never cross again so this behavior doesn't really require any explanation at all. Until, to your utter dismay, your mother yaps into the hotel phone a moment after it rings, "Colette. Colette who?? We don't have any Colette here!"

So there are secrets and there are lies but then there are also truths. Truth in advertising is all well and good, but truths in a novel like this? Just because this is a fictional piece of work doesn't mean it can't be spattered (spattered or splattered?) with a bunch of honest events and candid thoughts. Everything in a non-fiction book must be true but not necessarily everything in a fictional story must be made-up. There's no Literature Police to come along, prove something I've written is factual and haul my pages off to be shelved for life in the non-fiction section, or heaven forbid, the autobiography slammer.

Whether what I say is true or made up, I can tell you one person who won't ever peruse my writing again and that's my ex-husband. I was married to this man, (a true left-brained individual) for over a decade and not once could he read my story or poem without his red pen circling typos, grammar, and punctuation. I begged him to put aside the technical aspects and just read it for content—nothing more.

"Just concentrate on the emotion," I'd implore. "How does what I've written make you feel?"

"Terribly sad," he'd say and I'd think we were making progress. "Terribly sad that you haven't learned how to punctuate properly."

Another reason I want to give honest, personal accounts here is because I've heard the way to reduce stress and conflict is to be genuine with others, but most importantly to be authentic with your own inner-self. And I believe I've thought up an original way to achieve that too. So that this book will be both entertaining and amusing for you, yet therapeutic and cathartic (but not embarrassing) for me—from here on, my sincerest confessions will be mixed in with everything else. I used to write my diary utilizing this same method when I was younger. I was so terrified of what people would think of me if they found it after I died, that I invented details to integrate into my otherwise accurate journal. I'm the only one I know who wrote an entire diary under the assumption it would fall into the wrong hands.

To further illustrate what I'm attempting here, you know the ice-breaker game you play at parties? Everyone lists two truthful facts and one deceitful statement about themselves. People vote on which one they think is the lie. The more outrageous the declarations, the better the outcome. Here are mine:

1. I once spent an entire day submerged in a bathtub.
2. I was arrested for shoplifting.
3. No man has ever seen me naked.

My fraudulent statement will become apparent later on. Now I'm sure you can plainly see that along with changing my name in this novel, my friends and family members won't have a clue which parts are the true revelations and which events are slightly embellished or even entirely manufactured for dramatic impact and profit. Speaking of money, even if this book was loaned to you by a friend or you otherwise obtained it low cost or free, please pay attention to what I have to say. Not everything we pay a heavy price for is of value and not everything that comes cheaply should be discounted.

All the above should serve as an effective lead-in as to why I am at this very moment, hiding undercover, shuffling along a crowded shopping mall, and pushing a pink ruffled stroller that appears to contain the most adorable baby girl you've ever laid eyes on. But you probably need more of an explanation than what I've provided here—to understand why this one simple act is so dangerous.

Chapter 2

SONOGRAM HAS THE WORD SON IN IT

I hate backtracking, but sometimes it is good manners and becomes rather necessary, so here goes. My sonogram appointment was beyond a doubt, the happiest day of my life, even surpassing my wedding day and other births.

My appointment was at eleven o'clock and Nathan was late but readily forgiven because he stopped to buy flowers and champagne. Nathan is a physician (an eye surgeon) in the exact same building, so technically he could've still arrived on time. Dr. Grant was actually surprised that my husband took off work at all because he hadn't shown up for any of my other obstetrician appointments. But these past weeks, I've made sure Dr. Grant knew what kind of attentive husband I actually had. My conversations were peppered with reasons I was lucky to have such a thoughtful spouse. How he ordered me the highest quality prenatal vitamins online, handcrafted our own rocking chair, and then there was the time he took our sons bowling (which he detests) just so I could plan my baby shower in peace. And the reason he missed all our previous doctor appointments? Why, so he wouldn't forfeit any of his own patients and could better support our soon-to-be expanding family of six, of course.

"Well, this is it, Nordis," Nathan said as he sauntered into the room at exactly 11:11 am. That was a number I frequently saw on a clock (well, at least twice a day) and on receipts too and often wondered about its significance. Was it an ominous sign? A lucky number thing? But like most everything in my life, it was probably just my reading into things and it meant absolutely nothing.

Nathan wore his three piece suit that day, of course. Suits were Nathan's typical attire, even when he wasn't in his office. He liked to put forth a professional, formal image everywhere he went. He would look capable in his boxers. He stopped short of the table I sprawled on, eyes immediately riveted on the computer screen for any sign of movement from our baby. I was glad his gaze focused there instead of on my tautly skinned, freakishly over-extended abdomen, which was sticky with the Doppler conducting jelly that had been squirted all over it moments ago.

I scanned Nathan's expression to see if there was a hint of boredom or annoyance, having done this before. But no, his eyes were not glassy, they were bright and interested. Perhaps when you're an expert on vision, you can control your own eyeball behavior. I'd actually seen this look on him before when I hit a jackpot in Vegas or prepared his favorite stew—this was Nathan's enthusiastic face and so I savored it. I just thought maybe he'd ratchet it up from enthusiasm to all-out gusto, considering we both had so much invested in today's results. But with Nathan, you learn to appreciate what you get.

"Call Spielberg," Nathan said and pointed to the screen. "Looks like we've got E.T. in there!" Five years ago, during the embryonic stage of my twin pregnancy, he once remarked the image on their ultrasound looked like something you would dip in cocktail sauce. I chuckled nervously, but secretly thought this kind of humor was inappropriate and juvenile. Nathan was always joking, often the same punchlines over and over. If he had a new audience, I laughed heartily along with them, as if hearing it for the first time. That's what a good wife does, after all.

Following the joke, as a considerate afterthought, Nathan reached for my hand and his palm was far too warm for my liking. We waited. We waited to find out the sex of our unborn child. Nathan smiled.

And truly, what man do you know who would still smile after enduring four months of hell with an ugly, cranky, nauseas wife due to morning sickness which was the direct result of eight grueling months of sperm spinning? Sperm spinning is exactly what it sounds like. Only fortunately, they remove the sperm from the husband before they rotate it round and round in the mechanical agitator. I always picture the spin cycle on the washing machine or that paint toy kids play with called *Whirl-Art*.

"Centrifugation" is the technical term and it's the procedure used to separate the cute X-bearing female sperm which are said to be found in greater numbers at the bottom of the spun sample; while the Y sperm (those little macho tails) will hover closer to the surface. Several reports suggest sperm separation like this will result in over 85% accuracy in planning the specific gender of your baby.

Certainly far more precise than when I read that book, *"How to Choose the Sex of your Child"* to plan my last pregnancy. Since I had an eleven year old son, Michael, from a prior marriage, Nathan and I decided to do everything possible to sway our odds to conceive a little girl. After that, we agreed we would stop, having successfully completed our All-American family with one of each. I didn't exactly mention to Nathan that for me, it was far more significant than just balancing a tally sheet with offspring. But I diligently followed the female formula precisely the way the chapter outlined. I ate only things that would alter my body chemistry to be more acidic (favors girls) and not alkaline (more boys). This entailed not eating at restaurants and declining invitations with friends, which I willingly did because I prefer to eat alone anyhow. I always douched with the right concoction of vinegar and water just before sex. We never had intercourse less than four days prior to ovulation, and we always did it with the man (yes, the man was always Nathan!) on top. And most importantly, I never climaxed. The book says you can never do that. Ever. No problem. That was the easy part. The diet and douching were the hard part, but I knew it would all be worth it to finally have my girl.

Nine months later I gave birth to twin boys.

I won't lie and say there wasn't terrible disappointment during that period of my life. And yes, that was one of the many times my mother's medication opinion prevailed and I was placed on Zoloft for what was deemed an unfortunate but certainly understandable depression. Yep, that was a dandy idea. Take an already extremely disappointed, postpartum woman with double the hormones circulating in her bloodstream, wake her up twice as often in the middle of the night as new mothers of singletons, and then dope her up like a zombie. Wait, I almost forgot—make sure to repeatedly tell her the only thing that matters is her babies are healthy, full term and a great weight. Mine were born 5 lbs 9 oz and 6 lbs 2 oz, for heaven's sake. Now go ahead and figure out how much total baby weight I lugged around at the end. Interesting, isn't it?

The only thing that got me through this period was that our twins were utterly adorable and innocent, and they needed me. I also confess to loving the public attention I received when I wheeled them around in a double stroller—minor compensation. But my husband was amazing and that's really what carried me through. Right away he gave me his pledge—we could definitely try once more. And we would use science next time, leaving nothing to chance, Nathan had said. When I was ready.

I was ready. Dr. Grant began reading off measurements to his nurse. There were femur lengths quoted, the amniotic fluid assessed and placenta location estimated. I guessed what he was up to. He was purposely but good-naturedly trying to drive us mad, knowing which results we were anxiously waiting to hear but saving them until the very end. The results of all our carefully orchestrated husband and wife team efforts. Nathan's monthly trip to the lab to ejaculate into a cup, and my monthly trip for the painful insemination with the pre-sorted sample and all the frustration of . . .

"Jesus Christ, Grant, you obviously already know what it is, so just tell us for cryin' out loud!" Nathan erupted uncharacteristically. Ooh, a little passion lurked.

"Ah, but that's where you're wrong, Nathan. I wish I could help you out today but your baby is in complete control now." I looked at Dr. Grant questioningly. "Unfortunately it is not in the correct position for me to discern gender," Dr. Grant continued evenly.

The baby wasn't even born yet and already he or she (please she!) was calling the shots? I felt a surge of anger rise from somewhere within and both men and the nurse openly gawked as I, for the first time in my life, disregarded my normally self-conscious body image and started to shake, jiggle and maneuver my huge, bulging belly chaotically underneath the flimsy and now rattling paper gown.

Not finished with my efforts, I then hopped off the ultrasound table completely and bounced around the exam room with complete and utter abandon, all the while chanting, "Move baby, move!" Later on when you realize how insecure I am with my entire body, you'll know just how important this obviously was for me.

When I leapt back up on the table, the doctor and nurse had locked eyes knowingly (they probably knew I was going to burst from all the water they made me drink) while my husband enthusiastically high-fived me, then impatiently beckoned Dr. Grant to resume the position of the Doppler. There was complete silence for a few minutes and then Dr. Grant looked at me intently.

"I do believe you're going to get your girl."

I've never hugged anyone so hard in my entire life. I thought Nathan was even a smidgen jealous. But that's just not possible.

Chapter 3

Don't Look, Don't Touch

I have ruined many dates, three long term relationships, one marriage, and am heading into dangerous territory with Nathan over the same serious issues. The first one is that I don't like to be hugged. I don't like to cuddle. I don't like to be touched. And I don't like to be massaged. But I can be the toucher, I can be the hugger, and I'm told I give one hell of a massage. It just has to be on my terms.

First a quick answer to the obvious question that surely pops into most people's heads. No, I have never had anything happen that even remotely resembles being molested occur during my childhood. I was raised in a normal family—not overly touchy/feely but definitely not distant, cold or unaffectionate either. My mother was a stay-at-home mom and yes, I was physically comforted when I was upset or had the proverbial childhood boo-boo.

I have actually gone out of my way to pick men in my life who are macho and who, at least you wouldn't think, would have a need for this kind of physical contact. But each time after the sex or lovemaking (and I'm perfectly fine with all kinds of touching in that realm, by the way, so long as it stays within my designated body part boundaries) inevitably, they'll want to nestle up close and snuggle. A few of these guys, horror of horrors, actually think it reasonable that we sleep in this claustrophobic position all night long.

With their smothering arms, abrasive chest hair, their entwining legs, hot breath, and the involuntary twitching as they slip peacefully off to sleep with me as their hostage, I can't breathe. I panic. I extricate myself. I make excuses like, "I have horrible stomach cramps," or "I'm such a tosser and turner, you're better off like this, trust me." But invariably things go awry in other aspects of the relationship and most of their parting lines always sound the same. "You're such a cold fish," or "You really have problems with intimacy."

But am I? And do I?

I can connect with someone emotionally, passionately and spiritually on many different other levels if we're true soul mates. But they really have to convey that they understand and identify with me, spot on. (I hate that expression) That has always been the key for me. I have no problem making myself vulnerable and confiding in someone if the emotional chemistry is right. Aren't I doing it right now? Confiding that my skin crawls when someone touches me. Sometimes it actually burns. But always, it is physically painful.

Oh and yes, this sensitivity phenomenon happens around my children too. I can ruffle their little heads, pick them up, stroke their backs—I even rocked them to sleep every night when they were little. But if one of them approaches with that clingy "hip grip," I immediately try to distract them. "Oh listen, did I just hear someone knock at the door?" or "Have you finished your homework yet? Let's take a look at that spelling." If all else fails, I forcefully remove their little hands from my body part, because I swear I don't know what will happen if their groping continues. I do admit I've had the inexplicable urge to spank them but would never act upon that, of course. I can always talk sense into myself during these episodes and I've never lost control. I don't think I'm uncontrollable, just untouchable.

Privacy is also tremendously important for me so I've always been a big door-locker. My first husband actually dismantled the locks on our bathrooms when we were married to prevent me from bolting up. He claimed if there was ever an emergency and I passed out, how would he get in? C'mon, who faints from flushing? I think he just wanted to "accidentally" walk in on me naked.

No man has ever seen me naked. You can now eliminate statement number three from Chapter One's list. I know it's hard to believe and it's taken a lot of planning, I can attest to that, but my body has successfully remained a visual enigma to all of mankind. And I wholeheartedly endorse this kind of mystery between a man and a woman. I was born in the wrong era because my generation had "Let it all hang out" as its bumper sticker. But I would've fit in better during the 1950's when the old adage, "Some things are best left to the imagination," was popular.

I believe a woman's body, especially mine (and especially now) looks better at least partially obscured in the bedroom. There are all sorts of creatively seductive ways to remain modestly clad throughout even the wildest of times.

And I'm no prude. A quick paging through a Victoria's Secret catalogue should convince you I'm right. Teddies and camisoles, negligees and thigh-high stockings—these are the uniforms of girlfriends and mistresses. Why should wives have to give them up?

I know you think this is just a positive and clever slant in which to present my shortcomings and that clothing is literally my security blanket between the sheets. I can hear you now, "To truly make love to your man, you should be completely available and open to him without any garments to get in the way. And what about the romantic shower for two that's the prelude to hot sex? Or the shared bath that cements the bonding afterward?" Too much Oprah, nothing could be more disgusting!

As an aside, I also advocate personal grooming be done in private. That's why it's called personal. Therefore I never floss my teeth, shave my legs, apply deodorant or pluck my eyebrows anywhere near my husband. Brushing teeth is questionable too, but styling hair in front of a pretty dressing-table is permissible and can be a big turn-on. But the other aforementioned tasks cross into locker-room behavior and they'll just kill love. Unless you find athlete's foot romantic.

So I'll just say this—once you strip down, exposing your stark-naked body to someone, you enter the realm of medical exams and research cadavers and even concentration camp victims. And when you surrender that glamorous illusion, there's just no getting it back.

"When he sees it all, it fails to enthrall." I just made that quote up. Someone tell my mother.

I must end here because I'm actually typing this from a library instead of from my home computer, due to the latest argument over these issues with Nathan. And unfortunately, the librarian is signaling that time is up. I have a feeling when I see my husband, he might tell me the same thing.

Chapter 4

ONE THING LEADS TO ANOTHER

I worry a lot. I know there's some special medication I should take for that. But I worry that the medication hasn't been well studied and will cause cancer. One of my old therapists told me that the act of worrying is actually more likely to cause the cancer. My astrological sign is Cancer. I don't think that's a good sign. And it certainly doesn't seem like an accident either. Who names a month after Cancer? And then who has sex in early October, knowing you could doom an innocent child to be born under this ominous sign? I never used to even write the word "cancer" down, because a small part of me thought those particular letters in that specific order might be contagious. After all, nobody is quite sure how you get it. It's not only that cancer can kill you that makes it so distressing, it's that insidious, unstoppable things bother me. I just know one day I'll end up having something on my body that grows and grows without my permission, causing me endless anguish. Wait, I already did. My breasts.

    I can't say the word breast without thinking of breast cancer. I used to worry about breast cancer long before they came up with the statistic that one out of eight women will eventually get it. It just seemed like someone who had large breasts would stand more of a chance of getting cancer with all that extra tissue in the area. But after my reduction surgery, I felt my chances dropped down to the same as every other woman. I used to sit and look around during hospital ladies luncheons and wonder which one of us had it? Which one would get it? Which one of us already had it but just didn't know it yet? And which one of us would be grateful that having breast cancer was all she had to worry about?

It all finally got to be too much, and so I broke down and started my own women's support group. But it wasn't for cancer—it was for worriers. Now that I was pregnant and knew I was having a daughter, I didn't want to worry anymore. I posted a sign in our neighborhood community center and rented out the recreation party room even though there was nothing to celebrate. But maybe there was. I was reaching out. And more than that, I was reaching out to other women.

The first time nobody showed up but I had to stay the entire time since I was responsible for the room. I read a book called, *"How to Tame the Worry Monster."* It was a nice change from the usual *How to Raise Boys into Good Men* books I normally read. When the janitor came to lock up, he looked around and muttered, "Some shin-dig." But I didn't worry about what he thought of me, so maybe something had kicked in.

The next time around, I couldn't believe twelve women showed up for this brand new support group! I worried that I wouldn't know what to say to them. They had furrowed brows, pale skin and shaky, still, small voices. They seemed really concerned. Perhaps I should've hired one of my old therapists to come and run a professional group for us. But I didn't want it to be like that—so formal. I outlined my get acquainted, opening idea for the group—listing our top ten worries on a sheet of paper, then going around the circle and reading them aloud to see if we had anything in common to worry about. Before I could even jot down 'cancer' at the top my list, in sashayed a thirteenth woman. She asked if this was the Gratitude Workshop?

We stared at her. Her pale face glowed while her white hair sprang out in a jaunty-angled ponytail. She had no makeup on, wore white jeans, white tennis shoes and a white tee shirt, yet she appeared colorful. I looked past her, just outside to the Olympic-sized swimming pool where daddies splashed around with their children, throwing them up in the air and encouraging rambunctious, screaming behavior. Where were the mothers? In here? Shopping? A coffee klatch? Getting their hair styled? I remembered another time when I returned, freshly coiffed from the beauty salon and came to this pool announcing to Nathan that I was ready to take my turn watching the boys. The twins had begged me to come inside and play with them. Nobody noticed my new hair. And they knew I didn't swim. I suppose I physically could've done the breaststroke if I tried, but there was no way I would ever put myself in a bathing suit to see if I even remembered how. And it was blistering hot out. I remembered how the sun scorched my black blouse into my skin; I could feel the fabric melding to my flesh. Justin had started to splash water out at me, a fine mist of spray that seemed to sting my arm. I backed up, watching Jarrett douse Nathan with a bucketful of chlorinated water. Nathan just grinned and friskily shook his head, (like dogs do when they get hosed) then made that silly, childish brrrrrr noise where you loosen your lips, (just let them flap around) and the sound that comes out is really obnoxious. My hair would've been complimented if they had been girls, I thought. I touched my growing belly and thought how exciting it would be when she finally came out. Ava Rose. But then I realized that all the women in the room were talking and I (supposedly the group leader) hadn't been paying attention. I stopped staring outside and noticed there seemed to be a great deal of movement, commotion and excitement going on with the ladies.

The woman in white told us her name was Jane and suddenly we were all making a new list. We were writing down what we were grateful for. I sucked on the end of my pen. Of course at the top of my list, I had written, 'having a baby girl' but then I had to think of some more things to add. Oh sure, there were all the old standards but . . . too late. We were already going around the couch and reading our number one. The most important thing we were grateful for. The woman next to me read hers. It was the same as the lady next to her, and the woman beyond her. It was the same thing at the top of every woman's list in this room, "Having a healthy child" was the top reason to be grateful. I feel guilty saying this now, but at the time, I remembered thinking that wasn't the most important thing for me. I would take a sick child just as long as it was still a girl child. But I didn't have time to think about that in depth or weigh out the hypothetical "what ifs" (which I'm very good at by the way) because Jane was about to read hers.

"Orgasms."

Everyone got very quiet. Jane smiled, showing a row of stained, yellowed teeth. Didn't she know it was easy to get rid of that with special whitening strips these days? The other women in the room pursed their lips tightly and jiggled their feet. But slowly and surely, a discussion about sex had ensued. We didn't know each other and maybe that's why we could do it, but four women, including myself, admitted that we always faked pleasure in bed. Jane got truly riled up over this.

"How can you deny yourselves this immense joy?" she kept asking. "How can you deny your husbands?"

I knew my own reasons, but I was curious to hear the other explanations. One woman said she didn't want to hurt her husband's feelings, but that he did it all wrong for her. Another woman confessed she had never experienced "one" before in her entire life. Two others said it was always the end of a long day and they were just tired and wanting to get things over with. Soon, excited pandemonium broke out as private, animated conversations splintered off with two or three women relating to others their past sexual secrets. Jane watched and grinned.

I didn't speak, but instead ruminated about my own situation. Nathan was okay in bed, the problem was me. The lights had to be off, my negligee had to be adjusted, my angle had to be good, my hair had to cover my double chin and of course lately, my stomach had to be sucked in. It took so much of my effort and thought to make sure that I looked sexy, that I couldn't be sexy. How did Jane manage it? And with those teeth too.

The group ended up running four hours long and during that time we talked as if we had known one another forever. There was no cattiness, pettiness, judgment, competition or jealousy. It was the first time I had ever known the feeling of sincere sisterhood. We concluded by passing around a sheet where we wrote down our emails. I wrote down Nordis@yahoo.com and then thought about changing my password so Nathan couldn't read any of the girl-talk that came my way. Living in a testosterone heavy family, I've been deprived of girl talk. Thankfully that will all change soon. Anyhow, that afternoon when I had returned home from the support group, Nathan said the boys had missed me and wanted me to take them swimming.

The following week I arrived early for group, eager to set the room up and get started with my new friends. After everyone had trickled in, a handsome man poked his head through the door, looking a bit awkward. He introduced himself as Jane's husband and told us she was unable to attend that day—she had forgotten a previously scheduled doctor's appointment. For chemotherapy.

"She wanted you to know. So you wouldn't worry," he said and smiled.

Chapter 5

SUGAR AND SPICE AND . . .

Everything that's nice. That would be the easy way to explain why my entire life I've so frantically yearned to have a little girl. But by now you must realize I don't do many things the easy way. And the reason for that is because nothing seems to happen very easily for me. Most women can have a daughter without even trying. Sometimes it doesn't even cross their mind to have one and still they get one! It's this nice little bonus surprise for them that comes out of the blue (or pink). But not me. That stuff never happens for me.

If I want something really intensely, I can be sure whatever force out there that arbitrates these matters will give me the exact opposite of my desires. She wants to have shiny straight blonde hair? Give her bushy, unruly waves. And make 'em red! She hopes to one day marry a creative writer? Send her a technical engineer. I even attempted to trick this all-knowing powerful entity (I'm really trying hard to avoid religion here) when I got pregnant the first time by purposefully contradicting what I really wanted. I went around loudly voicing my desire for a son, pretending and reiterating to others how nice it would be to have a male child—an energetic little boy to toss a football around with at the park. But see, I went a little too overboard with my acting job because this great, omniscient, universal force knew I wasn't the least bit athletic and in fact, sensed I was the type of gal who got upset when I broke a fingernail. So nobody was duped by my theatrics and that's how Bingo—I got my first boy. Everyone called to congratulate me on attaining my heart's desire, of course. And my mother wrote on her gift card, "See, it's not nice to fool Mother Nature."

Most women are just content to have a child of either gender (which I admit is how it should be if you're going to become a mother) so long as the baby is healthy. There's that phrase again—the qualifier that's designed to instill tremendous amounts of guilt just for dreaming and wishing. I can't begin to count how many variations of the "just be thankful he's healthy" proverb I've heard throughout my childbearing years. And these are people besides my mother who recite this worn-out adage.

Okay, really! I do understand I'm lucky to have any baby at all, let alone a healthy one. But that's like saying you shouldn't desire anything precise or specific in life. "You shouldn't care what kind of house you live in so long as it provides shelter," and "Why are you so picky about which man you marry, just be grateful he has a penis." Aha! With the mention of a penis, we've come full circle in talking about the initial reason I wanted a girl so much. Girls lack penises. (Is that how you pluralize it? Or peni?)

Now, maybe my mother was remiss when she taught me how to become a good parent because she skipped over the lesson on how to care for that oddly-shaped but all-important appendage, the penis. And frankly, just thinking about that terrified the hell out of me when I was pregnant the first time around.

I knew there were things I would have to do with a penis. Swabbing alcohol on it (or was that the umbilical stump?) Wrestling with foreskin. Going into the public men's room for potty training. Since I'm Jewish, there would also be the mandatory circumcision. Now what mother could stomach the thought of that gruesome procedure on her tiny, eight day old, helpless infant? It triggers other issues too but I can't go into that.

I'll never forget when I announced my first pregnancy to my elderly and hard-of-hearing grandmother. After the initial congratulations and tears of joy, I remarked, "I really hope it's a girl so I don't have to deal with circumcision." She cocked her head and in her deep Yiddish accent said, "And what's wrong with serving chicken? So make a brisket!" That became Nathan's and my new inside joke. If you had a boy, you had to "serve chicken," aka circumcision.

A strong marriage should have a few inside jokes. Of course it's fairly easy to have a sense of humor about it the first time around because you know you'll get to try again and next time you'll get a girl.

But of course that wasn't enough for me. I had a need to know that I would definitely, for certain, be absolutely guaranteed to give birth to that little girl who lived in my mind's eye. The one I'd seen ever since I was four years old, when I played mommy/baby with my dolls (there was never a boy doll). She was the dark, ringlet-haired little moppet with long eyelashes who would be named Ava Rose.

Am I just an incorrigible control freak? Well, yes sort of, but I have learned to accept most things I cannot change. So why was the thought of going through life without a daughter so utterly heartbreaking to me? I didn't just want one because I thought it would be fun to dress a little girl up in those adorable frilly dresses or because I couldn't bear to part with my complete Nancy Drew book series, or I had a burning desire to see her walk down the aisle in my old, frumpy wedding gown. There was much more to it than that.

At first I thought the intense desire for a little girl came from not having a sister. When I was young, I used to long for someone to giggle with under the covers late at night, especially after watching the movie, *Little Women*. But that wasn't enough to create such desperation. Perhaps not having a close mother-daughter relationship with my own mother fueled my desire to have a daughter of my own so I could do it the "correct way."

I admit these are all the ludicrous theories that have been discussed in therapist's offices throughout the years to explain my obsession. One psychologist even insisted that having a daughter was all about my strong, unconscious desire to live my life vicariously through her—to watch her do all the things I never had the confidence to do and achieve grace in all the areas I was currently clumsy. Okay, I'm still tripping over that one. But I will admit I want her to have a small chest so she can turn a cartwheel without being knocked off balance.

Why can't it just be simple? I need a little girl. Period. Like I need water and oxygen. It feels like it has reached the point where I literally cannot live without mothering a daughter. But I'll talk about that desperation later on when I need you to understand the reason I do what I do.

So meanwhile, I continue to dream of tap-dance recitals, french braids, fashion shows and an enthusiastic shopping partner—those special mother-daughter moments all my friends with daughters got to enjoy when I gave birth to my firstborn son, Michael, seventeen years ago.

"Nordis, the ladies have all decided to plan a date for our *American Girl* tea-party at the Hilton. Would this Tues . . . ?" Their voices would trail off sheepishly.

"Boys can drink tea too!" I wanted to yell. It was like some club I was excluded from and the only way to obtain membership was to have a daughter.

My first little guy was wonderful, he really was, and I reveled in motherhood to the fullest extent. But when he toddled away in the park without looking back, I choked back the tears and remembered what my own mother used to recite to me as she polished my petite six-year-old fingernails.

"A son is a son until he takes a wife. But a daughter is a daughter for the rest of your life."

Chapter 6

A Mother's Work is Never Undone

My new friend Brenna (whom I'll speak much more about later because we gave birth on the exact same day and met in the maternity ward) just asked me if I ever do anything besides think of babies or write about thinking of babies?

The answer is yes. Believe it or not, when I'm not fixated on having a little girl, I channel all my energy and passion into other rewarding arenas. Like thinking up original business ideas that prove to others just because I'm not book smart doesn't mean I'm incapable of making money on my own.

I'm not the left-brained, mathematical, scientific type, which is about twenty percent of the reason my first marriage failed. The other eight-five percent is a long story. (I just purposely miscalculated that for my ex's benefit!) But as I told my then husband, (he designed chips that had nothing to do with salsa) "I may not be able to balance our checkbook to your liking, but just come to me when you need a poem written." And one day he did. I helped him write a poem for his new girlfriend.

My main problem is my enterprises are not very sensible, yet I never realize this until it's too late and I'm involved with thousands of dollars. Everything seems to make a lot of sense when I first envision it, but unlike most people, (who are able to logically think something through, and then discard it as non-viable,) I cannot discern practicality until I put my ideas into real life motion. At that point when my businesses fail, (as they were doomed to do from the beginning) I become disillusioned with everyone and everything. Sometimes I feel truly ill-fated or that outside forces are conspiring against me. Those are the times my mother tells me, "Things that sound good in theory don't always work in real life." Then she recommends medication.

There wouldn't be this tremendous let-down if I didn't sink my entire heart and soul into things from the onset. I get that from my father. When I dreamt up the idea for a video company that specialized in pregnant women, I was so excited that I practiced first on a friend who had to stuff pillows under her shirt because she wasn't even pregnant. The idea was a nine month service that ladies-in-waiting could sign up for that would celebrate their pregnancy with a custom movie set to music, *"From Here to Maternity."* It featured the parents-to-be announcing the exciting news to family, month by month close-ups of her growing tummy, ultrasounds, baby showers, picking out names, etc. The movie climaxed with spontaneous delivery room action, which fathers really appreciated so they wouldn't have to watch their baby through a viewfinder. Sad to say, I had to close down this business because each time the woman pushed out a little girl, my hands trembled so much I couldn't get steady shots of the birth.

Soon I diversified into the clothing business and manufactured a line of tee-shirts to be worn by new mothers. They were called "Activi-Tees" and featured shirts where the front had sewn-on rattles, squeakers, bells and beads, enabling the mother who wore this top to keep her baby happily engaged while sitting on her lap. She became a human plaything. These shirts were well received but poorly designed. Husbands pointed out that many of the toys were attached exactly where their wives' nipples were positioned, causing quite a stir when infants played with their mothers in banks or doctor offices. I didn't think they'd move their nipples, and it cost too much to rearrange the toys, so that was the end of that.

My next venture was publishing a book of "Preggo Poetry" which was rhymed verse meant to be read to a baby in-utero. The book came with a special microphone that brought the words straight to the ears of the baby as it was held up to the mother's abdomen. There were self-esteem enhancing rhymes like, "Dear baby fetus, we can't wait till you meet us!" or "We hope you're kind, smart and cuter than us, when you decide to emerge from that uterus."

I remember being proud that I rhymed the word uterus. But shortly after, I became disheartened and quit publishing poetry books because my former husband told people, "Sure, Nordis has lots of writing fans. They just haven't been born yet." Fathers-to-be were also shouting football scores into the uterine microphone, startling many babies and defeating the whole purpose.

Alright, so even I can see that all my business projects seem to involve babies and motherhood. It sort of happens for me that way. I go through periods in my life where I become the quintessential earth mother; grinding my own baby food, sewing Halloween costumes and crafting scrapbooks. Then without any warning, it all becomes too much, and if I have to brush one more set of teeth, I'll surely explode. Usually at that point I'm ready to unleash the other dimensions of my personality. And yes, I most certainly do have them—separate sides to me you'd never guess exist. Wildly, sexual sides.

Less than a year ago, in an effort to round-out my life, I impetuously began work at a telephone sex line. The phone calls were routed to my home number while my children attended school. Men dialed and I spoke with them about a variety of hot topics in my seductive telephone voice until they got off. They would then, in turn, cleverly inquire what time I got off? And when we could meet? Happily married for once, I was never really tempted. However, due to my client's "growing" satisfaction, shall we say, with my "services"—I was promoted to writing creative sex scripts for all the other females who worked at the firm. So when a woman purred, "Mmm, tell me more about what you do with that huge, stiff, hard shaft of yours," I was the author.

Ironically, this telephone gig led to a short term psychology job. It all started when a local philanthropist and prominent CEO of a major corporation (it wouldn't be ethical to name the company) called the phone sex line one evening. He was impotent, so even my best adjectives weren't working on him. However, he found me so compassionate, so utterly empathetic and understanding of his circumstance, that he invited me to join his new societal contribution—a nationwide crisis helpline. You may remember those 800 numbers you called for free (before budget cuts) when you were feeling blue, trying to conquer an addiction or perhaps even suicidal?

I thought the job was finalized but it turned out I had to pass a twelve week training course that was taught by several therapists before I could be recruited. Having been in therapy most of my life, I felt not only entitled to participate in the class, but perfectly qualified to teach it as well. I duly noted many of the unstable people in the class would be future callers themselves. Everyone knows troubled individuals are inherently drawn to careers in psychology.

At the end of the training, there was a screening process (which was a nice way of saying a big test) to see who actually would move on to the crisis intervention hotline in real life. The procedure consisted of sitting alone in a claustrophobic cubicle with a telephone. The phone would ring and one of the four therapists would pose as a troubled caller. You were given no advanced warning of the nature of the call and had to stay calm and proceed as per the training manual.

I fervently prayed my caller wouldn't threaten to end it all. What would I say? "There's so much to live for," sounded too corny and I wasn't sure I believed it myself. I rehearsed over and over all the appropriate responses

I'd been taught but when the actual phone trilled, I panicked and the entire training manual flew out of my head.

I recognized my caller's voice as that of the overweight, bearded therapist named Alan. He pretended to stutter and stammer and sounded quite nervous. His shyness put me at ease and as we conversed, my natural people skills kicked in. To my complete shock, my test call concerned sexual addiction.

"I can't stop thinking about doing this one woman," confessed Alan. "I want to give it to her seven, eight times a day." Why, this sounded like my phone sex job. I tried not to laugh, but the image of nerdy, short, portly Alan giving it even once a month to any woman was amusing.

"Is it interfering with the quality of your life, Sir?" I asked, knowing that was a key question in determining addictive behavior.

There was no response, just heavy breathing. I guess it interfered with his ability to speak. Boy, I thought, Alan sure was going to great lengths for realism. As I heard his panting quicken, I drew on my expert experience from my previous job.

"Are you masturbating right now on the telephone with me?" I grilled.

Again there was no answer except for the deep, guttural sounds emanating from the phone. I wisely remembered where I was currently employed and resisted the familiar urge to offer encouragement or egg him on.

"This is inappropriate behavior and our call is officially over, Sir," I said curtly and hung up. I held my breath as the partition door scraped open and out swaggered a pudgy and perspiring Alan. Would I be fired before I was ever hired?

It could've been my imagination, but I thought I saw his red face wince as he discreetly gave his zipper a tug before he spoke. "Congratulations, Nordis. Welcome aboard 800 Help-Now. You handled that like a true pro."

I'll never forget my first real call on the actual job. I conversed for hours with a soft-spoken surgeon who was distraught over his much younger wife because she was unable to stay faithful to him. He didn't know what to do because she was pregnant with their first child. I felt terribly sorry for his arrangement. He sounded like a man with kind eyes and I wished we could've met some time in real life.

Shortly after that, I was again promoted to writing the dialogue for the other phone counselors. It was in this peculiar manner, (between this and writing sex scripts,) that my interest in writing movie screenplays first began to develop. I would have to say that nowadays I consider this skill to be an essential part of my wellbeing. The ability to break life down into daily scenes and action as well as transform conversations I have with significant others into written dialogue really helps me cope and see things more objectively.

Have you ever had scenarios from your life replay themselves over and over again in your head until you've memorized every nuance, facet and expression? Sometimes there are blissfully happy vignettes like after the ultrasound when Nathan and I found out we were going to be blessed with a baby girl. I'll never forget the scene that followed in the children's department store as I ran like a kid myself, from display to display, babbling happy words to any sales lady who would listen to our amazing news. Nathan just chuckled to himself, encouraging me to buy out the store. Always superstitious, I carefully picked out just one perfect pair of little shoes—glossy, white patent leather Mary Janes, infant size two.

Sequences like that are so wondrous for me to relive in detail that I rerun them in my head numerous times. I have even used my skills to write times like this into script form so I can savor and relish all the specifics to my own heart's content. And I can show everyone else the lovely words on the page so they can share in my happiness too. See it in black and white? Proof positive that I am going to have a daughter!

Then there are those other types of events. Dark days that refuse to fade from that same slow-motion screen in my head. Those are the times when hope dims and reality blurs to just a fleeting glimmer of light. A tiny notion of dissolving coos and snippets of baby's breath are all that remain. Times like that are too raw to experience in the present moment, so I step outside myself and narrate from a distance. But the images and sounds of that metallic delivery room are etched forever as they flicker, flash and echo hollowly from the grim, cold lens in my movie camera mind.

Chapter 7

Making a Scene

INTERIOR—A STAINLESS STEEL LABOR AND DELIVERY ROOM—8:00 AM

This part of the hospital comes alive with the frenzied but happy bustle of activity that occurs when any new baby is about to be born. Efficient medical staff scurries to the beat of the baby's heart which blasts on a speaker, rapid and strong. Suddenly it ceases. That's because DR GRANT, renowned obstetrician, holds up a tiny and blood smeared NEWBORN. He says nothing. A well intentioned NURSE steps closer.

NURSE
Congratulations. You have a healthy little boy!

CLOSE UP: Baby's swollen genitals.

NORDIS, hair net on, droops back on table. Agitated.

NORDIS
What are you talking about? Please don't joke
about this.

Complete silence except for equipment noise which continues to hum loudly.

NATHAN
Honey. He's adorable. Wait till you see him.

Nordis attempts to lunge at Dr. Grant. A Nurse restrains her. Dr. Grant backs up.

NORDIS
No. How could you have done this to me?
You told me for sure. I counted on this.
My girl. My girl, my baby girl. Nooooo!

DR. GRANT
Let's give her a minute.

NORDIS
I don't need a minute. I need my daughter.
Give me my daughter. What did you do with
her? With Ava! Oh my god. What kind of sick
stuff happens here? Nathan! He switched babies!
Nathan!

DR. GRANT
Sometimes we see this reaction with the epidural.
And the joy of the moment is just so overwhelming.
The joy.

The nurses look uncomfortable and exchange glances. Nathan holds his wife's hand, and peeks around to watch the baby receive his first bath.

NATHAN
(Hisses in Nordis' ear)
C'mon Nordie, Don't do this. Look at him. He's
healthy. He's got your nose. And the boys will be
thrilled to have a brother. They can play doubles in
tennis. Please just look at him, Nordis.

Nordis props up dizzily on her elbows and looks at this baby for the first time.

CLOSE UP: NORDIS' FACE
Blank and numb.

Chapter 8

GROGGY AND FOGGY

With the birth of a new life comes the death of an old dream. It was all so real. The way it was going to be. Where do I file the vivid, color pictures that still exist in my head? I sit in the lumpy, institutional hospital bed and clutch the carefully chosen pink velvet and marabou trimmed "going home" outfit as I imagine myself proudly wheeled down the lobby corridor; the candy striper volunteers gushing over the tiny feminine newborn cuddled in my arms. There were tea-parties to attend, doll houses to build and ears to be pierced. Sweet sixteen parties to be planned and mother-daughter chats while sipping fru-fru drinks in hot-tubs discussing the wedding dress alterations. The mother-of-the-bride . . . will be someone else.

    I can't help but think of Halloween. It's early October and my last shopping trip to Target resulted in my boys begging for a sneak peak of their costumes. Traipsing through the sections of adorable girl shoes, girl hair ornaments, girl pajamas, girl toys, and girl furniture, we finally found our way to the "Spook Nook." And what a terrific selection we had. There were scruffy hobos, bloody vampires, tattered ghosts and masochistic pirates. But wait, that's not all—we could choose from every grungy, grotesque superhero in the world too! The entire time I browsed this department, my eyes sought out the delicate fairy princess, the exotic gypsy, the perky cheerleader and the graceful ballerina costumes. Oh how they beckoned me with their sparkly tulle fabric. Next year, I told myself—you will be buying one of these next year. But now the years will only be filled with tricks and no treats.

    My eyes start to hurt and I know it is because I wore my contacts lenses in the delivery room even when hospital personnel told me to remove them.

But I wanted to clearly see my daughter when she was born. Nathan ordered me these contacts a month ago and they've been two little disks of pain right from the start, burning and stinging my eyes.

The first person to call and congratulate me is my brother's wife. She's a wisp of a blonde with three daughters that she never fails to coordinate in matching sister outfits. She asks if they can visit me today and I imagine her parading the girls around the newborn nursery adorned in their fancy finery. My nieces will probably wear those gleaming pearl necklaces my mother gave each of them last Chanukah—while she gave my sons plain, brown cowboy boots. As I listen to my sister-in-law's cheery talk, I know that if I grip the phone any tighter, it will snap in two.

"Sometimes you can't force things, Nordis," my sister-in-law drawls on the other line. "You were meant to be the mother of boys. Raising fine young men to marry darling daughters like mine one day." What an incestuous bitch. I cover the mouthpiece so she cannot hear any emotion from my end.

"But you better chin-up mighty quick, my dear. You'll need all your strength to keep those wild cowboys in line on the range back home," she says. "I hear from your mother that he's a bruiser too. I'll make sure and buy the extra large overalls when I return these pinafores." I throw the phone and it clatters to a corner.

A kindly looking nurse walks in, probably hearing the racket. She looks from the tangled phone to my slumped figure buried in the sheets.

"We have your baby in the nursery. Would you like us to bring your child to you now?" From her awkward wording, I have a strong feeling Nathan has instructed the nurses not to refer to the baby as a son, a boy or a he. It's very considerate of Nathan to do this but it really doesn't help anything. Suddenly I can tell this well-meaning nurse thinks she has the answer to everything because she opens up her rosebud lips to add something more.

"Just think, you won't even need to buy any more baby clothes. You already have everything you need. Won't that be convenient?" I droop back down in bed and she furrows her brows. She's a nurturing do-gooder, you can just tell, and she's gearing up to make one last attempt with her tiny nurse-like whisper.

"There's a physician's assistant who works in oncology who can't get pregnant at all. She's had five IVF attempts. Everything is relative. You really are so very lucky."

My lips start to visibly quiver and my eyes brim full. I get some small satisfaction knowing that she'll feel horrible for making me cry like this. And she does.

She grabs the tray full of my untouched oatmeal and prepares to depart my room.

"I'm sorry Mrs. Spect. I thought I was helping. I obviously made a mistake."

That's it. She admits it. They have made a mistake. Any moment the head-honcho, hospital administrator will walk in here; a typical pencil-pushing, stuffed shirt who will clear his throat awkwardly.

"I run a tight ship," he'll state, "but let's face it, we're all human. Sometimes mistakes are made. The nurse who announced 'It's a boy!' has been diagnosed with severe vision problems. What she thought was a penis was actually very swollen labia. I'm sorry if she upset you. She told the last new mother in the delivery room, 'It's a kitten!' We're going to do something about her right away . . . maybe you can loan her your contacts or perhaps your husband can perform her eye surgery . . ."

"Oh, it's fine!" I'll reassure him. "I'm very understanding about things like that. Just bring me my daughter."

"It will be my pleasure, Mrs. Spect." He'll turn on his heel and depart for pink paradise.

I shake my head to keep myself awake. Why am I suddenly so drowsy? I'm being pulled into tranquil slumber, sucked into groggy dreams and yanked into foggy oblivion. If I sleep long enough, it will be tomorrow. And then it will be as if today never happened.

Chapter 9

It's Not "Weather" You Win or Lose

I hate sun. It feels good to say that. Okay, at this point in my story, you might start to think I'm losing momentum and am desperately searching for page filler by talking about the weather. Instead, let me assure you this might actually be the crux of everything so trust me—you don't want to skip this part.

I know that weather is a topic that people discuss on elevators and at the start of dinner parties before they're comfortable with one another. I know remarks like "Gosh, sure is a nice, sunny day today," make for safe and comfortable small talk. But sunny days are neither safe nor comfortable.

Just for a moment, suspend your belief about fair-weather days being beautiful and desirable. Songs in recent pop culture have actually brainwashed us to believe that. Try to forget the Beatles crooning *"Here Comes the Sun,"* John Denver raving about how happy sunshine makes his shoulders and little Annie belting out *Tomorrow*. The songwriters are in cahoots with the companies who market those special lamps for light therapy. And of course doctors get a generous kickback because they named the entire made-up affliction with a catchy acronym—SAD (Seasonal Affective Disorder). I'm not very political but I'm also working on a theory with how this all fits into the scheme of global warming.

My mother says I've always been terrorized by sun, heat and brightness. She had to order me special sunglasses to shade my infantile orbs because I would shriek and slam my pretty eyes shut in the daylight. But she refused to give up her bikini beach days. My mother is still, to this day, a sun-worshiper.

My heat aversion can also be traced from childhood when my brother caught colds easily and the doctors told my parents to keep the thermostat at a constant 78 degrees. This was back before they knew being cold doesn't actually cause a cold (viruses do) but nevertheless, it was so warm in our home, you lived in a constant state of undress—under duress.

During this time period most people wore only white undergarments (except for hookers) and so that became our family's standard indoor wardrobe. Only once our Kenmore washing-machine malfunctioned and the four of us were forever sentenced to be clad in dingy gray underpants (they didn't call them underwear then) and *Fruit of the Loom* undershirts. I can still see the large circles of wetness under my father's armpits when he changed the light bulbs in the kitchen's fluorescent ceiling panel. Sometimes a dead moth would flutter down and stick to his perspired forehead.

My own undershirt was sleeveless and had these tight little spaghetti straps on it which caused the fat around my upper arms to bulge and protrude on either side. My sniffling brother would come up several times a day, poke the excess skin there and say, "How ya doing Farm Arm?" then he'd oink like a pig.

I'd leave the house a lot to escape this scorching heat, but more often than not; it was warmer outside than inside our three bedroom toaster-oven. That's Southern California for you. The best days for me were cloudy with cold breezes. Outdoors, I'd delight that I could go bare-eyed but not have to be bare-armed. I was free, (without looking odd) because it was entirely justified with the nippy air, to wear sweaters or jackets to cover up my farm arms.

In a few years, it was more than just my arms and shoulders that needed hiding and I loved when it was what my mother deemed 'turtleneck weather'." But cool, crisp days were few and far between and that's why in climates like ours, prom dress styles are almost always strapless and exposing. But nobody remembers their prom night so you don't miss much by skipping. I know this.

Energy levels and body chemistry also fare much better in cooler, cloudier conditions. Have you noticed how drained you feel when it's hot and sunny out? Do you feel like going to the gym or do you just feel like vegging out (an insipid expression) on the couch sucking Popsicles? Do you honestly sleep well at night when someone grazes you with their damp, salty skin or does it jar you awake only to realize that drifting off again is futile because it's much too stifling in the room for any real dreams to emerge?

And once you're fully conscious and sweating, you know nothing interesting is going to happen in your muggy bedroom anyhow. It's a misnomer that people equate sultry with sexy. Look it up—more babies are born in August because couples only want to be close and get-it-on in the nice, cold, romantic, rainy Thanksgiving season.

So forget about *"Good Day Sunshine"* already. After all, which way do you feel more alive, invigorated and spiritual? Day after day, when you're handed the same identical blue skies and monotone sun? Or days when you're graced with these amazing dark clouds that hold the promise of variety?

Some days these clouds might bring sensual, wet sprinkles, other days bucketing downpours that make huddling under an umbrella with strangers quite enjoyable. Even snow flurries or hail could be thrown into the weather mix to make for some really remarkable elevator talk.

And there's always that chance you'll get a truly life-affirming, untamed thunder and lightening storm reminding you that yes, there really is something great and all-powerful up there.

Chapter 10

A Stitch in Time

The day after I gave birth, while Nathan and my mother went to the store to exchange things, I tried to walk. Mind you, I've done this a few times before, and with twins even, but it was never excruciatingly painful like this. I tore this time, and I think Dr. Grant put the stitches in me all lopsided, like he was in a real hurry to get out of there.

I hobbled past the nursing station and watched the women in white prepare baby bottles as they jiggled pink and blue wrapped burritos in their arms. They looked like they've worked here forever.

An older, authoritative looking nurse inspected a list then rasped to her cronies, "I need one of you in the north wing. 101 is doing just fine but 103 is a handful. I bet that dame was post-partum before she ever even conceived!"

I ducked back behind the opaque partition before she could see that I (the "dame" in 103) had overheard her. And how in the world could 101 be doing just fine? I had to know.

Room 101 looked bare and institutional, not at all like mine which swarmed with the enormous bouquets of flowers and balloons that Nathan had sent. A newborn baby girl, swathed of course in pink, dozed in a clear isolette.

A really young, first-time looking mother (Could this be the babysitter? Nah) sighed serenely in her sleep. And you could tell she really was doing just fine. I stood over her bed and tried to make my quick-paced huffing match her leisurely, dainty breathing. I ignored the feeling that something was leaking underneath my hospital gown and instead tip-toed closer to the baby. I might've liked to stroke her head.

"What are you doing in here? You belong in bed!" It was that old lady nurse behind me and she needed to clear her throat.

"I went to the bathroom and got mixed up. Came in here by mistake. They all look so similar, you know?" That was my seductive telephone voice.

"The toilets or the babies?" she asked smartly.

The baby girl whimpered in her sleep and the young lady in the bed startled awake. The nurse gave me a "see what you did" look but I ignored her and watched the new mother yawn instead.

"She can't be hungry again, can she? I'm too sore to feed her. Oh hi!" the girl said brightly in my direction. I was amazed to see someone wake up so cheerfully but I apologized to her anyway.

"Yes, she's very sorry," interrupted the nurse. "She came in here by an amazing mistake. But she's going back to her own baby right now." She started to guide my arm.

"Oh please stay and meet Bridget. Don't let that gorgeous bouquet of flowers fool you," the chiseled featured teen pointed to a dismal bunch of daisies on the night table in the corner. "Nobody's visited. My mom sent them because I think she wants it to look like I have a husband," she smiled sheepishly. "I'm Brenna, not Brenda. She also had a thing about hard consonants. My mom."

The nurse looked at both of us new mothers, one to the next, shrugged her shoulders with exaggerated aggravation and stalked out. I small-talked a little more with Brenna but realized I really was leaking something and it could be embarrassing. I excused myself and returned to my own potpourri-scented quarters. But I liked her.

Back in my room, there was an unexpected soft rap at my door and I knew that both Nathan and my mother would never knock, but I told whoever it was to come in anyhow. Maybe they were here to remove the stitches—the ones that evidently weren't keeping me together.

But it was someone whose name I didn't catch but who introduced her title as Patient Liaison. She squeezed herself between my floral shop, sat down gracefully in the rocking chair (which I thought was supposed to be reserved especially for me to nurse in) and began rifling through countless pages of notes. Minutes passed until she looked up, but that didn't intimidate me.

"It's very normal. You expected a baby girl," she murmured too kindly. I looked away. Okay, so here it comes.

"Nordis, that's a very unusual name. Nordis, can I ask what having a girl symbolizes for you?"

Oh, I can do this a lot better than you can, I thought to myself. You were just in grad school when I was already on my fifth shrink.

"It's just that I don't know how to be a mother to a son," I told her, crinkling my face up real ugly.

At this point she furiously ruffled through the paperwork as if she knew exactly what she sought and where it was located.

"But it says right here you already have three sons," she announced triumphantly.

"I have three criminals-in-the-making," I said, starting to feel real tears rising. "Two months ago, my seventeen year old lit a wastebasket on fire. And my six year old twins talk about stabbing our next door neighbor and stealing his Nintendo. Could they be growing up to become serial killers?"

"Boys will be boys," she said. Gosh, I'd never heard that one before. "You certainly have your hands full, but nursing your son will really help you with this bonding stuff. Breasts can be the answer to so many things," she said as she neatly paper clipped my papers and files together, then hastily stood up to take a perfunctory peek at the baby.

One parting coo and young Patient Liaison was gone, leaving me alone with my apparently Super-Smart Boobs.

Chapter 11

THE BREAST TEST

Even if I had wanted to successfully breastfeed that baby, I wouldn't have been able to do so. When I was sixteen years old, I had breast reduction surgery and they severed my nipples, putting them in a Petri dish. Of course they're back in their rightful place now but only about half the milk ducts reconnected themselves, which I think is pretty amazing at that. Please don't categorize this as one of those vanity cosmetic surgeries. It was anything but that. Insurance even paid for the whole thing because of my severe back problems, shoulder misalignment and scoliosis. And the fact that I was starting to give Dolly Parton some real competition.

I developed far earlier than I wanted to but it was one of those things I couldn't do anything about. I just threw up my hands in despair and watched helplessly as my body betrayed me with bosoms that quickly overflowed a C-cup at the age of thirteen. This was one traumatic period where absolutely nobody had any sympathy for me. In fact, the other girls shunned me as they chanted, "We must, we must, we must increase our bust," in gym class. Men my father's age were propositioning me in grocery stores and this was terrifying for me. It also caused a few scuffles for my Dad in the produce section by the cantaloupes. Who am I kidding? He'd deck 'em.

A triple D-cup at age sixteen, I watched all my friends get a job at a local printing company. I applied and was thrilled to get hired even though the owner's son never made eye contact with me during the entire interview. I was fired my first day. Two hours into the morning, I overheard the owner talking to his son.

"What were you thinking? The guys on the back presses are so distracted with her gazoontas they printed twelve books of page 30's. And when the

Berman broad came to pick up her daughter's wedding invitations, she asked if we're moonlighting as a massage parlor?" I felt my cheeks burn and the nausea rise in my throat but I dutifully kept stapling until they dismissed me, citing "uniform non-compliance." I purposely hadn't tucked my shirt in. It would've just made my freak show worse.

The surgery itself was uneventful, although my father protested my having it at all. He kept insisting to my mother that the way god made me was beautiful and nobody would be slicing up his little girl. When I attempted to show him photographs of what the surgeon would be doing he would mutter, "Dr. Mengele, Nazi bastard" and leave the room.

For my part, I had begged the breast surgeon to pat me down flat as a pancake. An A-cup would suit me just fine, I said even as I drifted under the anesthesia. But Dr. Stevens held firm to the belief that he would make me proportional to my body type and I ended up a generous C-cup. Nobody prepared me what to expect afterwards and when the bandages were removed, the upside-down T-shaped scars were really horrifying—red, raised and repulsive. But as awful as they were, they weren't anything compared to all the emotional scarring I had endured during the years that led up to a triple F-cup.

To be fair though, one scorching summer evening those grotesque scars actually saved me.

Telephone party lines had just emerged as the rage and the new way to meet guys when I was sixteen. You called a number and were merged with hundreds of other voices cross-connecting with each other, flirting, joking and trading personal information. I agreed to meet this one senior from another high school at the local Dairy Queen. Always on a diet, I didn't order anything but he asked me to a drive-in movie and it was *Saturday Night Fever* screening. My parents wouldn't permit me to see that film and I viewed this as a discreet way to disobey them.

We watched from the back of his pick-up van but right when John Travolta, (whom I had a mad crush on,) was in that disco bar ogling a stripper as she danced to that song, *"If I Can't Have You,"* this strong, pimply-faced stranger started pulling at my blouse. Firm in my belief about staying a virgin, I determinedly pushed him away. But he got stronger and meaner about it. He shoved me down and held both my arms over my head with just one of his powerful hands. With his other hand, he thrust his way under my skirt.

I thrashed and screamed but the scene in the movie blared and nobody in the other cars took a bit of notice. Suddenly he switched from my bottom to my top again. "Let's see those big, bouncy tits first," he slurred and I don't know why I hadn't smelled the alcohol earlier. He ripped the buttons off my blouse, lifted my bra up and in two seconds was dry-heaving, having glimpsed my recent scars.

"What the fuck? Are you some kind of a guy in drag? Like a transsexual or something. This is so gross!" As he retched, I seized the moment to climb over the middle seat and burst out the front door of the van.

"Good riddance, Fag!" he sneered loudly as I stumbled across the parking lot, patrons honking at me to get out of their line of vision.

I was grateful for two things during that film. The scars prevented a lot of grief for me because I sensed I was very close to being date-raped. But mainly, during that movie, I had been shown a sneak preview of just how a man might react to seeing the results of my surgery. I have wisely pre-empted any future performances ever since that warm, summer evening. Even though the scars have long ago faded, the scene from that drive-in movie still replays vividly in the cinema in my head.

It's odd that as a new mother, I can lounge here on our family room couch reminiscing about my teenage years while everyone else assumes I'm catching up on some much needed shut-eye. Long ago, I learned if you close your eyes and hold still for a long while, people assume you're sleeping and will talk about you as if you're not even there. That's when you can find out what they really think of you.

I become aware that my houseguests (a few close girlfriends and their husbands who came to admire the baby) are conversing with my mother and Nathan. Someone just asked how much weight I gained. How come when you're pregnant, your weight becomes public information?

"Oh, Nordis will drop that baby weight quicker than you can say 10K race," Nathan says confidently and I grimace at the thought of having to go back to my grueling jogging regime. "She's naturally skinny. Eats like a bird," he adds proudly and I recognize how his voice sounds with a handful of cashews stuffed in his mouth.

The others murmur their agreement and I wait tensely to see if my mother will interject the secret she knows about my past. But she behaves herself and instead recites one of her famous quotes, "Count your blessings, but count your calories too." The guests snicker.

Hearing her say that, I start to realize how much I've enjoyed the pregnant reprieve from my normal food restriction. It's so liberating being able to eat what you want and having people actually encourage that. Now that I've given birth, it's back to stringent food rationing. I envy actresses who must gain weight for a movie role as I imagine their agents and producers must applaud every pound gained. How relaxing that must be.

I hear the baby fidget in his Moses basket from the floor and immediately I can tell that my mother responds, picking him up. Through the din of the background talk, I hear her whisper to Nathan.

"Don't you think you should start her tonight? Remember last time."

Good god, will she ever stop with her antidepressant campaign?

"I'm keeping a close eye, Judith. She's holding her own, all things considered," Nathan says.

They must've moved away from my sofa because their voices fade and now I can hear three of my gal pals talking so clearly, it's like they're on speakerphone. I can't help wishing my new friend Brenna from the hospital was here instead. Even though she's only sixteen, I feel as if we're connected somehow. But I listen to my three girlfriends converse instead.

"A bit odd she hasn't named him yet, doncha think?"

"You know, one of us should offer to return all those shower presents."

"I think her mother already did. Or at least I heard she changed the nursery."

The nursery. It was the pinkest, frilliest, loveliest sight you could ever imagine for a darling angel girl to grow up in. I know, I'm aware I haven't even dropped a clue as to my own physical appearance yet, but please indulge me as I describe the nursery. That's all that's left of it—my words.

No photographs could be snapped, no video could be filmed, and no friends could be ushered through for an "ooh and aah" tour because my mother came in and systematically dismantled the whole adorable sight under the guise it would be kinder this way. Missing in action was the "Welcome Home Ava Rose" banner I had the party store personalize. The empty frame that said "Future Ballerina" obviously experienced the same fate.

No doubt my feet still straddled the metal stirrups in the delivery room when the white lace eyelet canopy was torn from the crib and in its place—a muddied color denim bed-bumper was installed. The pastel satin butterfly mobile was replaced with dangling cowboy boots. The wall border I had meticulously hand painted by tracing Xeroxed copies of pink carousel ponies had been painted over and bright red bandanas covered the space. Yippy ky yeah, I hate western.

She also took it upon herself, my mother did, to return all of the delicate dresses, the spring bonnets, the satin piped anklet socks and yes, oh yes, she even discovered the shiny white patent leather Mary Janes hidden in the closet under the quilts. She disliked those from the start.

"Over indulgent and over-the-top," she had admonished. "Nobody buys shoes until a child is walking." But there was a whole other stack in the laundry room, waiting to be de-tagged and washed that I bet she hadn't happened upon yet.

I hear the clink of glass and our unruly friend Roy Clark moves into my earshot.

"Samuel Adams! Now that would look nice on a birth-certificate. Howya doin' Sammy boy?" I cringe as I picture him with his beer breath, chucking the baby's chin. "Wanna night cap? Hey Nate! Wake that wife of yours up and let's make a little titty toast." I crack my eyelid in time to see him raise his beer bottle high.

"Nordis isn't going to breastfeed," Nathan states awkwardly. I can feel everyone's searing eyes turn on me as I struggle to keep my own lids from quivering.

Chapter 12

BABY FACE

And he does have the cutest little baby face. I'm not a callous, heartless mother; please, please believe me. But understand this is IT for me. It was our last try, our very last chance to have a daughter. Nathan made me swear we would be done. Actually, the previous time with our twins was supposed to be our official final attempt, but Nathan was compassionate enough to see how important this was for me and so he let us have one more shot at it. I just can't bear to go through this life never experiencing that mother-daughter relationship. And after the ultrasound, it was so real. She existed. If not yet in this world, then vividly real in my head. My little daughter. I saw her on the screen. Whatever could have happened to my little girl?

On the outside I'm going through all the normal motions of motherhood; I'm fixing my other kids breakfast, packing lunches and getting ready to bathe this baby. But on the inside I'm screaming loud, agonizing, pathetic cries of anguish. But I can't let anyone know what I'm really going through because absolutely nobody understands this kind of pain. I need to find a way to express myself, so I close all the blinds downstairs, every last shade and curtain. I want the house dark and somber to reflect my mood and to show our respects for what has happened.

I am in mourning. Mourning for the baby girl that died when this baby boy was born.

Nathan comes downstairs, all polished (I look a wreck) and ready to go to work in his stiff suit. He's just searching for his briefcase and then he'll be off. I consider hiding it. I don't want him to leave. Might as well be honest about that.

"Can't you just take one more day, Nathe? I feel really funny. I feel different. I don't think I'm bonding." I set the baby in the motorized swing and look pleadingly at him.

"Your mom will come over later. Look through the name books. That'll help you. Let's narrow it down. My vote is for Charlie."

Justin, one of the twins, trots into the room chewing gum. He heads for the refrigerator, "Charlie, Charlie, Bo Barley . . . hey, that's a cool name," he says and his bubble pops.

"I still don't understand," I press on. "Tell me again how Dr. Grant said this could've happened?"

"Nordis, we've been all through this. He said sometimes this just happens. His little uh, thing just wasn't showing up clearly on the sonogram. Obviously not from my side of the family!" Nathan snickers.

See, I think to myself, it always comes down to a penis problem.

But aloud I say, "Yeah, I know. I know. He claims it was tucked in. Tucked. Let's just name the kid Tucker for god's sake." I force a wry smile to show I'm still keeping my sense of humor.

"Tucker, Tucker Bo Bucker. Banana Fana Fo Fucker," sings Justin, then he spills his milk. Neither Nathan nor I make any attempt at wiping.

After everyone launches off to their various landing zones, I sit at the kitchen table and stare at this baby. I try to feel a connection. The connection. What I should feel. Therapists have told me not to use the word should. Okay, what I want to feel. He's a hearty baby. He wriggles his arms and legs vigorously.

Ironically, he's got truly lovely features. No hair though, he's a baldie, but gem-like green eyes with heavily fringed lashes. I was always told I might carry recessive genes for light eyes but they've never surfaced until now. There's the standard baby nose but the chin is unusually shaped and remarkably sculpted, like an artist chiseled it out of alabaster. Who in our family has this kind of chin?

My mother comes in our front door using her own key. She has said she needed her own key in case of emergency and Nathan copied one for her. I scrutinize her chin. No.

"It's like a morgue in here," she announces as she methodically walks around the house, twisting blinds, parting drapes and yanking shades until they snap up to the ceiling—letting the sun surge in. "There! That's much nicer. Don't you think?" She knows what I think.

I busy myself wiping up the spilled milk before she can see it and comment.

"So where are you headed?" she asks, eying my packages.

"I'm bringing all these maternity clothes to Karen," I fib. "She's pregnant again." Karen, Nathan's sister really is pregnant but that's not where I'm going.

"Oh, good for her. That's nice of you, she's been through so much trauma. I heard she remarried and I know how long she's wanted a baby. Any baby," she emphasizes.

"Yes. Well he's asleep and I expect he'll stay that way until I return so make yourself comfortable." I'm politely casual.

"He whom? Does he have a name yet?"

I jostle plastic bags loudly as she speaks so it's as if I haven't heard her. I'm gone.

Once in the boutique, I recognize the woman who helped me register for my baby shower. She was a real "Talking Tina" and today I don't intend to pull her string.

"Hi, I remember you! You were so fun to register. A bunch of your friends came in and bought out the store. How was the shower? When was she born? What did she weigh? Is she adorable? Where is she?"

Breathe, I think, but I'm not sure if I'm talking to this nutcase or myself. I make perfect little piles on her counter from all the stuff that was stacked in my laundry room. All the adorable things my mother thankfully, never noticed earlier. Oops, there's that little personalized bracelet with lettered pearls, "Ava Rose" that my Aunt Carol had custom made for my shower. Guess I'm keeping that.

Chatty Cathy looks dismayed to see just how much merchandise I'm returning. Probably her commission is at stake.

"What . . . ," she stammers. "Why, she must be an itty bitty thing. You can get all those items smaller, you know." In response, I simply shake my head no.

"Oh, a little porker, huh? My daughter was over 9 lbs too. Well, we'll just trade 'em up for the next size. Girls clothes are so much fun, aren't they? Especially prom dresses."

Oh yes. Prom. I had forgotten. I was already planning a beautiful sleeveless dress that showcased her slim arms. But nobody remembers their prom anyhow, I think, and pull out my credit card, ready for this nonsense transaction to be over with.

"If it's a matter of not liking them," she persists, "well, we just got a whole new line in over there by the window. Go take a looksy. Pink rosebuds."

"I had a son," I say this softly as a single tear glides down my cheek.

"Oh. Oh. Well, what do doctors know, huh? Besides boys are so sweet. All those snakes and snails and rat's tails." She talks as she walks and heads to a back corner of the store where I thought only the rejects and clearance clothing were hidden.

"Puppy dogs," I say but she doesn't get it.

"Well, here's our wonderful selection of boys' clothing!" She points to a single depressing rack of dark blue shirts, pants and one piece outfits that say, "Lil Slugger" or "Sailor Boy" on them."

"Thank you. No."

"Well, at least keep this sweet little hat," she says and I gently accept a cap back and pensively finger the soft mint green material with the little furry lamb on the side.

"It can go either way, girl or boy," she proclaims. That's the first sensible thing said to me in a long time.

Chapter 13

ZEALOUS AND JEALOUS

I can't explain why, but it has always bothered me that my husband never gets passionately crazed if he sees someone flirting with me. Who am I kidding? He doesn't even get mildly miffed. It's like he somehow knows that a smile, direct eye-contact, and a touch on the shoulder between me and another stranger will amount to absolutely nothing.

Nathan is so secure with himself that he never even blinked an eye when I announced I was working for that telephone sex company. It's nice to be trusted, but why doesn't he worry someone could actually desire me enough to put the real moves on? And that could lead to . . . to what?

I do get a little worked up on this subject, so forgive me. But, the point is Nathan doesn't get worked up over any subject. Just once, I would like to see a little intensity from the man. He's so even-keeled and logical. My mother adores this about him.

"He's so established, Nordis," she said when we married. "He'll balance you."

Then she'd compare Nathan's stability to my father's fiery character, god bless that man. I didn't like her doing that and always wondered who really came up short in the personality department. Fire equals passion and passion means you care about something or someone.

Bottom line, shouldn't the thought of losing their wife to someone else make most men just a tad bit jealous? I had to find out if Nathan was like most men. Two years ago, I did.

It all started when my sister-in-law Karen (Nathan's sister) told me she had taken her wedding ring off due to swelling during her sixth week of pregnancy. When her husband Paul found it, he became terribly upset and insisted she put the ring back on. He accused her of wanting to feel single again and asked her if someone had already approached her in the dry-cleaners that day. She laughed nervously when she told me this anecdote, but I think she was secretly thrilled someone loved her this much.

That very evening I slipped off my own ring as I did the dishes and then walked away, leaving it in plain sight in a soapy puddle on the wash basin. An hour later, Nathan gave me the wedding band back with an admonishment that it wasn't insured and to be more careful.

Of course the next day, a finger-traced message appeared in the foggy back window of my mini-van that said, "*Can't help Falling in Love with You.*" Any guy in the neighborhood could've easily written it as he passed by. That's entirely plausible. A lot of men on our block see me jogging. I waited for Nathan to discover it but he never did, so I pointed it out to him.

"Oh, you romantic guy, that's so sweet of you to do that," I said with mock surprise. I waited.

"Huh? I didn't do that," he said. "I hate Elvis." That was it. That was the entire reaction. So I had to continue with the script.

"Well, if you didn't write this, then who did?" I prodded.

"I don't know Nordis, but this car is filthy. Remind me to take it in this weekend." We both went back inside and I wondered if he'd wear his suit to the carwash.

That night our phone rang twice and when Nathan answered, they hung up both times.

"Damn kids," Nathan grumbled. I scurried into the next room but he shouted for me to come back. Maybe something was having an effect after all.

"That's a very pretty dress. Is it new?" he asked. It was one he picked out for me as a mother's day present just this past May.

Before long an email came to my account from an address called, *HotForYou@Anon.com*. There was one sentence, "I'm waiting, watching and wanting you!" I actually thought that was pretty clever because it sounded sweetly romantic, but at the same time bordered on a little bit of a mischievous, thrilling tone.

When I shakily summoned Nathan over to the computer and motioned to the screen, he warned me to be very cautious and report it immediately. At first I was touched that he'd show such concern. But then he told me he'd heard of a scam where women who masquerade as men online, send flattering emails to lonely, older, wealthy ladies to get to their money. Especially the wives of busy doctors and lawyers.

"So this could have been written by a woman," he said triumphantly. Hmmm.

That's when I knew I had to go for a run. If Nathan wouldn't become insanely jealous over me, perhaps he would become fiercely protective of me. I made a big production of putting on my jogging shoes and mentioning how dark it was that night because the moon was stuck behind the clouds. When I returned breathless and pale, I recounted how a large, dark male figure had chased me through the canyon in our community center.

Nathan gave me a hug because I was shivering and proceeded to tell me a long, involved story of how one night he was in grad school walking back to his dorm when, because of a strange case of mistaken identity; someone pursued him all along a shadowy path by the library.

"A stalker with a doctorate degree," he laughed at his own joke.

Before he could finish or explain why he would relate this incident at this particular moment in time, the doorbell rang right on schedule and a delivery man from the local florist held out a beautiful bouquet of brightly colored roses in every shade of the rainbow with my name typed on an envelope. The card read, "For a dazzling, colorful woman."

"From your mother," Nathan said. "Probably to apologize for mentioning to her bridge club that you should start antidepressants again."

"I don't think so," I said. "My mother knows things that die quickly really depress me."

"I didn't know that," Nathan said. "All those Valentine's days I've brought you flowers."

"Nathan," I said worriedly. "What if all these things that have been happening are all related and someone is after me. Like foul play?"

Nathan then told me three things. He loved me very much, I should write mystery novels and that indeed I was dazzling and colorful. We went upstairs, I donned my black lace teddy and we had sex.

In the middle of the night, I slipped out of bed and pulled open a box I keep in the closet with some of my father's belongings. I skimmed through his yearbook and saw how many people wrote messages like, "To the wildest guy, never allow yourself to be tamed," and "I'll never forget how crazy you got over Violet May. Hope college brings you all that passion and more!" or "Keep living your life on the edge!" Then I read an apology card he had sent to my mother saying he was sorry about yelling and throwing his dinner, but when she came home so late, he was insane with worry and love for her."

Something glinted from the bottom of the box and I picked up his watch; a watch that to this day nobody knows I own, because I had slid it off my father's wrist before the hospital workers kicked me out. I hadn't wanted to share it with my brother. I headed downstairs with the timepiece and noticed it still ticked loudly.

I set the watch gingerly down on an area rug where people wipe their feet. I quietly opened the front door just a little bit, so it was not really ajar but not really closed and locked either. It was in that in-between stage.

I slept in late the next morning because of strange dreams that had disturbed my slumber most of the night. But the twins jostled me awake, bounding under the covers and exclaiming, "Mommy, mommy, the police are here. The police are here."

"Maybe they heard you guys talking about strangling Jake next door," my eldest son Michael taunted and grinned from the doorway.

"The police?" I sat up blurry eyed and held my nightgown a little tighter around my body.

"Nordis. We've had an intruder," Nathan said as he came in. "Come downstairs immediately to help me make this report."

I never went down because I was extremely sick to my stomach all morning. Nathan told me he would change the locks and stayed close by my side the entire day. He even said we should cancel our evening plans going out to the karaoke club with his sister Karen, and Paul. But I felt a distraction was needed and so we got a sitter and went.

Nobody in our foursome sings except Paul. It was so crowded that he only got called up to do one song. He crooned, *"Can't Help Falling in Love with You,"* by Elvis Presley.

As soon as Nathan recognized the familiar strains of melody, I observed him sitting tautly upright in his chair. Several times it seemed like Paul made direct eye contact with me but it could've been Karen since we were sitting so close together. When Paul returned to his seat, I asked if anyone knew the time? Karen pointed to Paul's empty wrist and asked why he didn't wear his watch?

"I lost it," he whispered and I saw Nathan's jaw clench just a little. We all left then because I was tired, my stomach still hurt and besides the guys already had enough to drink. Nathan dropped me off and then went to an all night pharmacy to get something to help me. I think he had it in his mind to prescribe me something.

The next morning I got a hysterical call that Paul was dead. Karen had gone to bed early, tired from her pregnancy and awoke to find Paul on the living room sofa, lifeless. I later heard the shock caused her an immediate miscarriage. When I frantically reported the news to Nathan, he told me that Paul had asked to talk privately last night and he sensed there was something going on with him. We hugged each other tightly, grateful to be able to do that, I suppose.

"Did they find a note?" Nathan asked.

I hesitated. "I never told you it was a suicide," I said oddly.

But there had been a typed note discovered next to Paul, vague and cryptic. Nobody has spoken of it since. It said, *"Can't help falling in love with you."*

Chapter 14

PAT THAT HAT

Shopping at the grocery store with the baby and my twins, the boys insist on unloading the food all by themselves onto the moving conveyer belt. They drop cans of corn on the floor. I straighten the baby's special mint green hat so the fuzzy lamb faces forward. He dozes lazily in an infant carrier attached to the cart. The cashier waits patiently as I dig inside a stuffed diaper bag for my credit card.

"I want that," says Justin.

"No gum," I say firmly.

"I want that," says Jarrett

"No lifesavers," I say, knowing the routine.

"That," they both point and chime in unison.

"No razor blades," I say on auto-pilot. "Maybe next time."

The female bagger has been staring at the baby. She reaches to pat the hat.

"What an absolutely precious baby girl. You're so lucky to have the twin boys first and then the daughter," she says. "It's what I'm hoping for. Boys first so they can protect their little sister. And then she can date all their friends when she's older. Right, boys?" She giggles. The twins ignore her.

"Thank you," I say and take my receipt.

"You're welcome. Enjoy her. She's perfect."

"I will," I say and walk away, elated.

The boys plead for a visit to the park and since it isn't too warm out, I don't see the harm. As they dig merrily in the sand a few yards away, I lay the baby down on a blanket. I look around and discreetly pull out a pink satin headband that I never returned to the store that day. I finger it gently and then nonchalantly stretch it over the baby's bald forehead. Just for fun. Just to see. Just because I've never gotten to do this before.

Two girls suddenly appear from behind a tree, one with heavy metal braces on her teeth and the other one with the worst case of teenage acne I've ever seen.

"Oh look! How old is she?" Metal Mouth bends down to take a closer look at the baby.

I hesitate and look at the twins who are out of earshot.

"She's almost three weeks."

"I've never been this close to one so young. What's her name?" Metal Mouth asks in awe.

"Ava Rose."

"Ooohh," both girls fawn.

"If you ever need a babysitter, I'd love to." This is from Acne.

"How about right now?" I ask impulsively.

The two teens look at one another, astonished. I snatch up the baby, the headband and point to the sandpit.

"They're six. They won't give you any trouble. There's juice in this backpack. Be back in one hour. Thanks!"

I scuttle off before they change their minds about doing this . . . or maybe before I do.

Back at our house, I consider calling Brenna first. She's the only one that seems to understand me. But then I ask myself, what could a 16 year old, first-time mother know about something like this? Instead I sloppily throw clothes, diapers, stuffed animals and some snacks in a large duffel bag. I look wild-eyed around the family room, mentally searching, then dive into the toy rubble after spying what I'm looking for. A child's blackboard.

I scrawl with a broken piece of chalk, "Pick up twins at Moonlight Park. Don't worry about me. I've gone on a short trip to bond with baby." I hastily prop it up against a large teddy bear, then I grab the baby, my bag, and open the door. I glance back inside the room one last time and scramble back to chalk, "P.S. I love you."

Chapter 15

COLDER AND BOLDER IN BOULDER

There's no question where I'm headed. Just last night, Nathan and I argued for the umpteenth time over the heat. He thinks 75 degrees is room temperature and when I'm not looking, keeps nudging up the thermostat a few more notches and adding a few more comforters to our bed. That doesn't make things more comforting. Perhaps I mentioned earlier how oppressive and stifling I find heat to be? And if I go outside for a breath of fresh air, it's 86. So I can't be inside and I can't be outside and there's nowhere in between.

I need to go where people understand all this and where they thrive in cool, crisp, clear-headed weather. Colorado.

Ruthany, (although everyone calls her Ruth) my best friend from high school and all throughout college, lives there in Boulder, and she and I have both related to one another during the years with our mutual strong desire to have a daughter. She was not successful because her husband felt that interfering with what Mother Nature or god intended was wrong. I don't think I'm going to like this man all that much; he sounds rigid and judgmental. Anyway, they have a newborn son named Caden. I know this because I received the elegant birth announcement a few weeks ago. I never sent my own announcements because I had to return the lavender parchment paper, but now I can't wait to show Ruth in person what I've finally accomplished.

The baby is well-behaved on the plane ride, (a little doll actually) and I remember, as I chew my own gum, to give a bottle on take-off and descent for the ears. We rent a car and it comes with a carseat already strapped in which is brand spanking new, pink and white floral.

"This is much prettier than our old hand-me-down," I say to the rental clerk. "Ours had to go through a set of twins." She smiles and watches me toss my shabby seat in the trunk of the car.

As I drive, I tell myself that everyone deserves a temporary break, a little reprieve now and then from real life. Isn't that why they invented vacations and sick days? There's no harm done and Nathan will probably be glad to focus on his clients a little more as I've been insisting he come home early to eat dinner with the family. My mother will surely encourage him to stay late while she dines with the kids. After all, she supports his stable career.

I'll take just two weeks off. But they'll be the best two weeks of my life. Nobody knows me here and I can experience what having a daughter is like in peace and harmony. It occurs to me that in Boulder, there will not be the urgency to "drop my pregnancy weight in no time" as Nathan had said. I won't have to take up running just yet either. People won't be watching and scrutinizing my figure. And my well-meaning mother won't say, "Bigger snacks mean bigger slacks."

So, going away is actually a triple bonus. Not only do I get to escape the heat, but I get to eat normally and most importantly, have my daughter too. After it's all out of my system, this much needed indulgence, (wrong word, indulgence is for whims and this is quite necessary) I'll return home refreshed and go back to dealing with my life as the same overheated, dieting mother of four. Four BOYS, I remind myself. I really like outlining these details in my head because then things don't appear haphazard or impulsive. And it truly is shaping up to be a good and organized plan, especially for someone like me.

We stop at the mall to get a few necessities and I must say this is a most enjoyable shopping trip for me. Now that I know there are beautiful green eyes to accent, I take particular pleasure in picking out the cutest pair of ruffled emerald jammies, a lime colored onesie with bows scattered all over, and a solid mint colored dress. But enough green! The rest I buy in my old favorites, pink and lavender. I confess the entire reason I'm stopping at this mall is to replace the pair of Mary Jane shoes and the very last store is where I encounter them. They are perfect, delicate and shiny. I total about $450 in two hours. Lastly, I pick-up several boxes of Twinkies at a drugstore, stare in brief amazement at the cash register total, $11.11 and we're off.

Even though this is supposed to be a nice hotel, it still seems dumpy and depressing. The room is suffocated by all my baby supplies and there are no shelves for me to display my books, including the one I just purchased, "Traveling with Your Newborn." I also miss my kids. For a split second I think I could be making a mistake but then I have another little common sense talk inside my head. I remind myself that I know more than other people (including the "experts") about what helps me cope. After all, I am me and they are not!

And in this case I need time. Everything was too sudden. The loss was too sudden. With my twins, at least I found out before they were born and had the time to ease my mind, gain some perspective and prepare for reality. Even Dr. Grant had said, "Give her a moment," in the delivery room which proves that shock is difficult on people and time is clearly needed to help with the shift in mindset. When people say "a moment," they don't literally mean just sixty seconds though, and I'm sure Dr. Grant would approve of a couple of weeks recuperation.

I tear open a Twinkie from its plastic casing and look at the baby. Ava Rose. I should get used to that. I can't have a baby with no name and that particular name will fit how I plan to have him dressed while we're here. I should just get used to calling him "a her" as long as we're in public too. There's so much I've always wanted to pass down to a daughter, I think. Private mother-daughter discussions. Since I only have two weeks, I better start talking right now.

"Okay, here we go. I've devised a way to weed out the liars of the world," I say aloud. "The insincere individuals who act as if they like you. You know, you never really know what someone truly thinks about you, until you leave the room. Or pretend to fall asleep. But that's not always practical, so here's what I do sometimes, and you can do this also. When you grow up, that is," I tell the baby who looks at me and yawns.

"What I do is I tell a joke. A joke with no real punchline. Then I carefully watch for their reaction. It's my human litmus test. Don't ever trust the ones that laugh. If they laugh, they're phony baloney. Honest, straightforward people will admit right off the bat that they don't get the joke," I say and then stuff an entire Twinkie in my mouth. "This is exactly how I fell in love with your father."

But the baby doesn't appear to be listening and has, in fact, closed his/her eyes. So I'll just tell you, (because I hope you're still listening) how I met Nathan. In fact, you're used to my style now so let me give you a flashback scene. Because it really is so very memorable for me.

INTERIOR—A CLASSY BAR—EVENING

A YOUNGER NORDIS and a MALE MODEL TYPE sit next to each other at an art deco bar. Male Model has his hand on her knee.

CURRENT NORDIS (voiceover)
Remember the joke isn't going to make any sense.

YOUNGER NORDIS
. . . And so the doctor says we could have avoided that if only you had some mustard!
A pause.

MALE MODEL TYPE
(Cracking up)
Oh, that's great! I can't stop laughing.

ANOTHER CLASSY BAR—ANOTHER EVENING

Younger Nordis sits at a dark mahogany bar, this time with FOOTBALL JOCK.

YOUNGER NORDIS
. . . if you just had some mustard!

Football Jock elbows Nordis roughly and nearly falls off the barstool with his unruly laughter.

FOOTBALL JOCK
Too funny! You are one, too funny chick!

STILL ANOTHER CLASSY BAR—YET ANOTHER EVENING

Younger Nordis on a double date, sits in private booth near a stained-glass bar with two guys and a woman.

YOUNGER NORDIS
. . . Mustard!

Four faces burst into hysterics. The laughter is WAY TOO LOUD as Nordis looks away.

NOT SO CLASSY BAR—FINAL EVENING

A younger, but now weary looking Nordis sits in a dingy, quiet booth, this time with a younger looking and terribly handsome NATHAN, wearing a suit, vest and tie.

Long, awkward silence.

YOUNGER NATHAN
God! That was awful. You're the worst joke teller I've ever met. What does mustard have to do with anything?

YOUNGER NORDIS
Let's go back to your house.

    I become aware there are a lot of Twinkie wrappers littering the hotel room floor at this point. But it says right on the box, "wholesome goodness moms can trust," I enthusiastically tell the now awake baby, "We gotta trust Hostess." I hold out a golden sponge cream-filled delight. Of course he doesn't take it but he does bat spastically at the box.
    I turn the television set on with the remote and it blares a scene I immediately recognize from the movie, "*Tootsie*." The baby and I watch as Dustin Hoffman applies make-up for his transformation into a woman.
    I smell something and realize the baby needs a new diaper. I'm a little shocked when I unwrap him and see um, well I see that he's definitely all boy. It is funny how caught up you can get in fantasy. But I remember I've always been quite good at playacting. My mother still likes to talk about my imaginary friend Tilly when I was five and the fact that she had to bring her dinner on a separate plate when she served mine.
    So, yes, being confronted with reality can be a bit startling, however for tonight (when we visit my old friend Ruth) and for these next two weeks, (I turn to the baby when I say this next part in a high, squeaky voice) "We're going to indulge our nutty mommy, aren't we?" It seems to me the baby nods approval, but probably not.
    Still, this is very positive. I recognize I'm talking and interacting with the baby a whole lot more since we've been on our little trip and that has to be a good thing. Right?

Chapter 16

Wish You Were Here

I'm drained from the plane ride but as soon as Ruth hears I am in town, she insists I bring Ava Rose and come right over tonight. I feel uneasy. I haven't seen Ruth since I was twenty three. In high school, she was always the popular drill team girl. We both wrote for our school newspaper, but she had an alluring photo of herself that used to appear next to her articles. The last time I saw her, we were snipping hair at a local salon, putting ourselves through college before we each got engaged. We've talked on the phone lots and I still feel close with her but I wonder if that will translate into good girlfriend chemistry in real life. Like I now have with Brenna.

I miss Brenna and decide to write both her and Nathan an email. The high cost of the hotel room includes unlimited computer internet and that's worth it to me to stay connected. I purposely forgot my cell phone at home so communication will always remain in my court.

Dear Brenna,

I'm on a little soul-searching trip right now. Just the baby and me. I decided some time away would help with all the things you and I have talked about. How is little Bridget doing? She is so darling and I know I sound like a broken record but something about her really reminds me of when my eldest was a baby. Anyhow, I hope your mother has eased up a little bit and accepted her place as a grandma even though she wasn't expecting it. Believe me, I know how mothers can be and I'll share more about that in my next email. Speaking of family members, if my husband should contact you while I'm gone (it's doubtful, but he might) please remember to keep all our conversations confidential and I will always do the same, I swear it.

Love,
Nordis

The next one will be much more difficult. I need to watch my tone and my language because I know it will get forwarded on to my mother. It needs to sound light, breezy and totally and completely emotionally healthy.

Hi Nathan,

I miss you and the boys so much but this one-on-one time with the baby is really helping me. It's exactly what the doctor ordered. Sorry I didn't say goodbye in person but you know your spontaneous wife! There was this amazing plane fare posted online and I couldn't pass it by. Give the boys a big hug from me. Tomorrow I'm taking the baby and we might see the sights, maybe even Mickey Mouse.

Love and kisses,
Nordis

p.s. I'm liking the name Charlie more and more so I think we've got a winner!

I'm hoping the Mickey Mouse mention makes him think Florida, just in case. I don't want to be found before the two weeks. This is my special experience and nobody is taking it from me a day sooner. The baby has drifted off again and I take advantage of the quiet to style my hair just perfectly. A little beautician trick—when your body isn't looking its best, make sure something else looks stunning enough to distract the eye. In this case it's my hair. The red color is already quite eye-catching but when I lift it up and swoop it over to one side, it's possibly enough to keep people from looking at my figure below and seeing . . . Twinkies.

I rehearse everything about tonight. I even think about telling Ruth that Nathan and I had a horrible fight and that's why I've come to Colorado alone. That would justify going out of state and validate why I don't want to be found. But my life is getting complicated now and I don't believe another lie will be necessary. Ruth won't think it strange at all. She's very independent and I'm sure she takes separate vacations from her husband all the time.

In two seconds I know I'm wrong. The phone jingles and Ruth confirms that I'm still coming but then relays that they just came home from dinner to a strange message on their machine. It is a man saying he's my husband and that I have gone missing and he has no idea as to my whereabouts. He's going through my phone book (I should have taken that with me) and calling everyone to ask if they've seen me, Ruth finishes reporting, sounding astonished.

"Don't call him, Ruth," I say. "I'll be right over but trust me, if you care about me, don't return the call."

We hang up and I'm in a panic. There's nothing to do now except put the cutest dress I own on Ava-Rose and slap some make-up on me. I remember back to my cosmetology training and I'm confident I can pull this off. I mix a little purple, dark blue and muddy brown eye shadow, then swirl it together with just the lightest touch of black. The perfect shade for a bruise.

Chapter 17

SIGHT FOR SORE EYES

I stand on the doorstep of Ruth Manning's beautiful colonial style home and think she's really done well for herself. I've heard from people at our class reunion that her husband is an older but exceptionally good-looking breast surgeon. I take a deep breath and ring the bell, hoping this goes okay. I'm not really even sure why I let her know I was coming into town to begin with. I could've said nothing and she never would've known. But deep down I know why. I had wanted someone, just one person who knew me, that I could show off Ava Rose to. Because that would make it more real. I hear rhythmic, clicking footsteps on wood and the door is thrown open.

"Oh my gawd! Nordie! Look at her. She is just too precious! Come in you two girls. You're used to L.A. weather. You can't be left standing on a cold porch!"

I step in awkwardly and embrace teeny, tiny Ruth. How the heck can she look like this so soon after giving birth? Our babies are only two weeks apart! In the light, I can tell she's seen my eye but she makes an initial effort not to stare.

"I tried to keep Caden up but he fell asleep," she apologizes. "But they're so close in age, we'll get them together while you're here." Then she doesn't waste any time. "Nordis, WHY are you here? Why doesn't Nathan know you're here? And what in gawd's name happened to your eye?" She points to my left eye.

"Oh Ruth," I begin on cue and look down. But then I remember I shouldn't look down or she might too. Keep them looking at my wild, distracting hair, that was the idea.

"What does it look like happened? Remember I told you he was so even-tempered? Well it turns out that was just a good cover-up. One night he started yelling and he hasn't stopped since. This last time he completely lost it and hit me." I lightly touch my eye for emphasis. "It could be sleep deprivation . . . she keeps us up a lot. But no excuses. I always knew if he crossed the line from yelling—I'd walk. So you see, he can't know where I am. Promise me you won't call him." I end with a flourish of my hands. I know Ruth and from a past incident at our hair salon, I know this will resonate powerfully with her. But I look around the corner wondering where her husband, Sam is. I have to extract a promise from him too or I'm sunk.

"Good girl, Nordis," Ruth takes me by the arm just as I'd anticipated. "Let's have tea alone in the den. Sam will just have his guy point of view and we don't need that right now. Nothing male. Just us girls. Right little Avie Rosie?" Ruth picks up the infant carrier by the handle and leads the way.

We pass by a large, heavy marble statue—Michelangelo's David. Ruth leans close to its ear. "Hear that? No boys allowed!" She sticks out her tongue and waggles her finger at the enormously tall sculpture. I giggle nervously.

Halfway through our girl talk, Sam knocks politely at the den door. He's far older than I thought and dressed in casual jeans and a tee shirt, he doesn't exactly portray the image of an esteemed surgeon. He's not even fantastically good looking like I'm expecting either but for this I'm glad. I don't like too perfect. I feel as if I can't be myself. I have a hard enough time being myself under normal circumstances. Ruth looks too perfect, even after all these years and it's really embarrassing for me. Hell, it's mortifying. After all, Sam knows we've both had a baby at the same time and here's his drop-dead gorgeous wife and then here's me, Miss Shlump.

But then a little, tiny, bright thought creeps into my head. "I got the girl!" I tell myself and secretly smile inside. And that was something Ruth really wanted. And I know what that kind of disappointment can feel like. Wanting something with every fiber of your being and in the end, you don't get it. I start to feel really petty at this point and begin to tell myself I should actually feel sorry for Ruth, not envy her. But Sam interrupts my thoughts, which I somehow know should be interrupted because they're getting a little convoluted. It's late and I'm tired from the long trip. Why am I even at these people's home, anyhow? I excuse myself to go to the bathroom.

"Right around the corner," Sam says. As I leave, I hear Ruth berate Sam for not dressing a bit nicer. This could be intriguing.

I walk out the den door, tap my own heels a few feet on the wood floor, but then remove my shoes and pad silently back to listen outside the door.

"You see that eye?" Ruth is saying. "He beats her to a pulp."

"Ruthany, you shouldn't be gossiping. She'll tell me what she wants me to know."

I think I really like this Sam.

"Her little girl looks so happy and smart," Sam says, obviously changing the subject.

"I think she's rather homely. And look at that bizarre chin."

"If she's in town for any length of time, I'm thinking of our apartment building on Fern Street," Sam murmurs.

"Oh Sam! She can't run that building. She was always really poor at math."

"I'm sure she can, Ruthie. It's perfect. We need a manager and she might need some money and a place to stay. It's the perfect job for a mother."

I accidentally graze the doorknob with my sleeve and it rattles.

"Shhh, she's coming," Ruth hisses.

I walk in and tell them their powder room is lovely.

"Oh, but it's so plain," says Ruth. "Sam prefers me not to wallpaper or texturize the walls. Not even a little crown-molding."

"Sometimes simple, uncomplicated things are best," Sam says and looks directly at me.

I decide to do it. To tell my joke. But first I sit down.

"... and so the doctor says, this never would've happened if you had a little mustard!" I conclude, pause for effect and then smile myself to get them started.

Ruth titters exaggeratedly and ends with an odd sounding chortle. "Oh, Nordie, you always were quite the comic," she says.

Sam stares back at me, looking completely confused. "Maybe it's me," he says. "Tell me that last part one more time. I'm not sure I get it."

"Oh Sam!" Ruth swats at the air between them and her long, magenta acrylic nails glisten. "You never get anything. Never mind him, Nordie. It's late and we're all tired. But the day after tomorrow? A walk along Boulder Creek?"

I nod and ready myself for departure. When I hug Ruth goodbye, she whispers in my ear that Ava Rose is the most gorgeous baby she's ever seen. When I hug Sam goodbye, he whispers in my ear that he actually does get a lot of things.

But it's late, and I might have imagined that.

Chapter 18

WORTH A THOUSAND WORDS

As I remove my black eye with Pond's cold crème, I wonder where baby is supposed to sleep. I've just found a note on my door apologizing that all hotel cribs are currently in use. I'll have to give this issue some thought but first I think about what I would like tomorrow to bring. When your days are fleeting, you want to make sure each one is filled with as much joy as possible. I have thirteen left. Since it's been determined that we're spending time with Ruth the day after tomorrow, I plan on fulfilling a longtime fantasy I've had just as soon as I wake up tomorrow morning. Taking a mother-daughter portrait.

Photographs are very important to me. Videos too. They facilitate memories. Without your memories, you cannot be sure something actually happened. Because once it occurs, then it's over. Done, finished, gone. Without a photograph, there is no proof. Photos help things continue on. In a photography class I took years ago in college, I was proud of this one concept photo I took. It's simply a picture of the class instructor holding a picture. But the picture he's holding is again of himself holding another picture. And that photo depicts him holding yet another picture. And in that picture . . . well you get the idea, so on and so on, forever, infinity. A concept I really love but also one that scares me. I only received a B on the project because the instructor said I overexposed his hands.

My very favorite activity to do with Nathan is reminisce about the first time we met one another. What we were each wearing, thinking, drinking, etc. I have clear, vivid memories. He wore a three piece charcoal tweed suit, ordered a dry martini, up, with two olives, and thought my quirky smile was extremely sexy. I know that last part because he's told me. Lately when I've tried to talk about that first date with Nathan, he seems to remember less and less. Last time he couldn't recall what I was wearing, and I had to be the one to tell him what he was thinking. Doesn't exactly bring the same feeling of gratification. Maybe if Nathan had a photograph of us from that night, it would jog his memory of the event. Because if Nathan forgets, who will I have to walk down memory lane with? If Nathan can no longer remember, then who can confirm that we really did meet at that bar? That we even met at all.

Back home, I have tons of scrapbooks, photo albums, and memory boxes filled with photographs for each of the kids. Even the twins have different ones because, well, they're different. The albums always begin with the delivery room snapshots. Every angle, every position and every emotion are captured so I'll never forget. I draw my breath in quickly when I just now realize I have no memory of Nathan taking photos this last time in the delivery room. I have no memory of it because it never happened. Nathan forgot the camera. But the worst thing is that nobody remembered that Nathan forgot. And a couple of years from now, it'll be quite likely Nathan will forget that he forgot. He could even blame me. Because none of it is officially documented. This poor baby. He/she has no pictures. We will make up for that tomorrow.

I sleep with the baby in my arms throughout the entire night. It is only done for safety sake because there is no crib or barrier for the bed. Sometimes I startle awake because I am not accustomed to having someone clutch instinctively at my skin. He is overly warm, but tonight, a little clamminess isn't too hard for me to deal with.

Tomorrow comes and because there is an hour wait for our photo session at The Portrait Place, I am able to stroll through the mall and find precious mother/daughter outfits in the Laura Ashley store to wear in the studio. I'm normally not a floral pattern type person but it's worth it to have this bonding experience. I also brought from home that special pearl bracelet with "Ava Rose" on it (one letter on each pearl) and I clasp this around his/her dainty wrist. People see me carrying the baby down the main corridor of the mall with everything matching between us and they keep smiling and making wonderful, beautiful comments that I can't help but hear. I don't want to forget what they are saying. I don't want to forget this day. Soon I will make a memory of it.

I carefully print names on the sign-in register at The Portrait Place. I've stopped writing in cursive ever since handwriting analysis became popular. Too risky. I don't use our real names though because I'm being very careful about not leaving signs or clues as to our whereabouts. Just in case. We are Meredith and Melissa Markowitz. I am feeling in an M & M mood today.

There are many terrific poses taken of us. My favorite is a soft, feminine shot with the baby in my arms, wrapped in a white, feathery marabou boa. We are looking into one another's eyes. The photographer tells me he does modeling portfolios as a sideline and would we be interested in posing for some professional mother/daughter pictures that could possibly be published? I think hard about this but in the end, decline. These are private and personal memories.

When we return to the hotel, I check my email while the baby snoozes. I'm a little worried that this baby sleeps so much and it could be an illness. Brenna's little girl was sick before I left and the doctors were running tests. One of the symptoms was sleeping an unusual amount. I'm not sure how they knew what an unusual amount is though because babies sleep a lot normally. I tell myself not to worry. If I wanted to spend my next twelve days worrying, I would fret about this lump that seems to have appeared on my left breast. But I don't want to obsess and agonize. That was my back-home behavior.

When I log on, I am surprised to see the first email in my inbox is from Jane. I think fondly back to her and my women's support group. I open her email.

Dear Gracious Nordis,

It's really nothing.

Love,
Jane

I'm perplexed by this email but I don't take too much time to think what she could mean because the rest of the emails look pretty scary. I had anticipated as much after Ruth told me Nathan called there, so I purposely didn't go online before today's photography session. I didn't want my smile to look phony in the pictures because I am sincerely happy right now. The next email is from Brenna who writes far more maturely than her sixteen years. It even crosses my mind it might be someone else posing as her in the email.

Dear Nordis,

I am so glad to hear from you! I wish I would have heard from you before your husband phoned me though. He is very worried about you. He asked me a lot of questions and I'm afraid that I did give him some answers after he told me you and your baby's welfare could be at stake.

He says after every pregnancy you go through an unusual amount of postpartum difficulty and it is apparent to him now that you definitely need to be on some medication. Nordis, please call me as soon as you get this email. I am going over to your home tomorrow night to meet with your husband.

Hugs,
Brenna

P.S. Bridget isn't gaining any weight and the doctors don't know why.

My body cools down a little after reading this email and now Colorado seems to be a bit too chilly for my liking. I'm even more hesitant to open Nathan's email.

Nordis,

If you don't contact me as soon as you read this email, I'm afraid I will have no choice but to go to the police. What exactly do you think you are doing abandoning me and the other children? What is it I'm supposed to tell them again? That their mother went to Disneyworld because she thought Daisy Duck would give her some tips on motherhood? Bring our baby back home immediately and we can get you some help.

Please call me now!

Nathan

An icy feeling runs through my limbs and Colorado seems freezing now. I look out my window to see if it has begun to snow. It hasn't. I think what I'm feeling is extreme dread. I am scared of what Nathan will do or what he's already done. Abandonment? Why would he use a word like that? Next thing he'll be tossing around kidnapping verbs. Doesn't he understand that I'm doing what's right for me and the baby? It's helping, not hurting. Besides, many working mothers go away for a little while on business trips and everyone survives no worse for the wear. I dislike how some people can always make me question myself, what I know and what I believe. I touch the lump in my breast and hug the baby. Yes, that's definitely too much power for anyone to have.

Chapter 19

"Grate" Expectations

I'm stuck. I can't leave the hotel and I'm worried I'll be late for the walk with Ruth and the babies. It is actually the most ludicrous thing that's occurred, but not really too absurd if you take into account that it's me we're talking about. As I sleepily diapered the baby this morning, my elbow bumped my rental car keys. They fell off the bureau, and went straight down through the heating grate in the floor. I've called the front desk and they said they are sending someone for assistance. The only thing is I don't know who they are sending. I wanted to ask if it would be a man or a woman. Are key retrievers male or female? Why does this even make a difference? It makes a great deal of difference for me—it always has. Especially if I'm going to be alone in an intimate environment with this person for any length of time. It's the awkward factor.

The first item of concern is my weight. Men and women evaluate that so differently and you've got to be really careful. Women can be snarky with their sideways glances, sucking in their own abdomens so the comparison is in their favor, and their egos get a boost. But then there are some men who act like they don't notice a thing but then can't wait to go home and tell their wives about the woman they saw who would be the perfect candidate for the "Flatter Stomach in Thirty Days" video.

Luckily now with a baby, I've got a valid excuse because nobody expects you to be back in shape with such a little one in tow. I remember Ruth from the other night and feel those familiar twinges of envy. How did she get her figure back so quickly? Ruth didn't comment on my appearance, but I know she was thinking I've really let myself go. And I have. But keeping myself up takes such a huge amount of effort these days and I'm so tired. I just need a little time off from the many required tasks involved with a woman's mandatory daily upkeep. Why can't our society just relax the standards of how we're expected to look just a little bit? Especially as we age. My life would be so much easier if I didn't have to worry about being judged on a daily basis.

The first thing I do is straighten up this mess of a room. I'm disorganized by nature and the truth is when I'm alone, I thrive in a chaotic environment because it's not so sterile and I can relax and let my creativity flow. But right now, I hastily jam all the fast food wrappers and cellophane from Hostess into my suitcase. I would never just offhandedly toss it in the open wastebasket because someone could easily peer inside and make the assessment I'm just a junk food junkie. People do stuff like this, believe me. They form opinions in less than thirty seconds and you've got to be really careful what you present them with or be prepared to deal with the shame. The disgrace of partaking in any kind of self-indulgence. Just another reason I prefer to eat privately at home and not in front of others in restaurants. People watch what you order on a menu, especially waitresses, and you've got to have an explanation ready to fire off like, "I'm celebrating getting a positive pregnancy test," which is always a valid reason, and then people not only approve of your lack of discipline, they actually encourage it. But more often than not, you can still get away with making an insightful statement like, "Oh, just this once, I'll be naughty and make up for it later," when ordering a quesadilla with extra guacamole. That's deemed permissible as well, so long as you're careful not to say it too often around the same tablemates because they might just conclude that you binge and purge, which I just happen to know a little something about.

I certainly hope they don't send a woman up here to assist me. If a woman comes up here and I'm alone with her, I have to be prepared to make conversation about typical things that interest females, which I'm not very good at. It would be especially nerve-wracking if it's that one head front-desk clerk, Audrey. That real fashion plate in her late twenties with the drop-dead figure to match. I noticed she checked me out when she checked me in. There's a sort of snooty condescension about her that I sometimes detect in certain women of that age. Women who haven't had children and have absolutely no idea what child-bearing can do to your hips. I can always feel Audrey's eyes on me, appraising what I'm wearing when I pass by the reception area. But it's easy to stroll by for just a moment with a polite nod because I always have my coat and boots to cover me up, and the baby's frilly frocks always distract and elicit little niceties from her coworkers.

But if Audrey actually comes up here, she'll have built-in scrutiny time and that's when I never seem to measure up. Especially with other women. Especially doctors' wives. Although, I do happen to know when the Nordstrom sale begins and that's always an intriguing small-talk opener. Babies are always convenient for a few choice observations and lighthearted remarks, but if they're sleeping like mine happens to be, then there's not much to say. Just in case, I ceremoniously lay out my one good Kate Spade handbag on the already straightened bed. (I make my bed here, even though I never do at home because I don't want the maid to think I'm a slob.) I invested in this one exclusive purse a while ago, so even if I'm not correctly put together the way the others are at the hospital ladies fundraiser luncheons, I still have a fallback item that makes me acceptable. And you don't have to be thin to make a purse look good either!

You can see why it exhausts me to be around people. All the preliminary planning that has to go into it.

Now, if it's going to be a guy coming up here, I have to figure out what to wear that not only sends the right message but definitely doesn't send the wrong one. Although truth be known, it's far easier to dress for men because they just like bold color. There's no real designer label concern on their part or appalled expression if you're wearing something from last season. But you have to be careful with any mannerisms that could be considered provocative. Last night, I saw this young, good looking janitor whose nametag identified him as "Van" coming out of the room next door with a toilet plunger. That's certainly embarrassing, and I'm terribly grateful I only have a key/grate issue to worry about this morning. But I cannot be late for Ruth.

I'll just bet someone like Van gets a lot of lonely, older women summoning him up to their room with silly, transparent ploys. Wait a second—car keys in a heating grate sounds pretty flimsy and preposterous. Will he think I'm trying to seduce him? I think back on the Mrs. Robinson scene from the movie, *"The Graduate."*

Oh my god, that's probably Van right now! I startle at the rhythmic knock at the door—he's pretty musical, I think. And I better snap together this one last button so there can be no question about my blouse status. On the other hand, with a sleeping baby I'm probably pretty safe from any roguish janitor's advances. All at once, I feel a little tingly, nervous and excited as I move to let him in.

When I open the door, I'm surprised to find both Audrey and Van standing together, a little too closely, in my opinion, for projecting a professional image.

She giggles coyly and he seems to be flexing his muscular arm around a long pole, which is what I assume, will be used to retrieve my keys.

"Excuse us, Ma'am," Van says as he enters my room without even a look up in my direction. Ma'am? That's quite the assumption, isn't it? I'm alone, I could easily be a Miss. He might as well just say, "Step aside old, fat slob."

I decide to hide out in the bathroom but first I caution them that a baby sleeps in the corner and not to bump her. I remember to say "her." They don't make any comments on the baby and in fact don't seem to notice anything except each other. From the bathroom sink, I can overhear their murmurings.

"Watch out, you might poke the television with your long pole," Audrey giggles.

"You oughta see what else I can poke with my pole."

"Mmm, is that right?" Giggle, giggle. "Sorry about last night, baby." Now there's whispering and kissing noises which really irk me. I slide my finger under my bra to check on my lump. My contacts pinch my eyes. I can't wait to have these well-dressed, youthful, tanned, wrinkle-free people out of my personal space.

As they both holler that the keys are on the bed, I realize Audrey never even noticed the Kate Spade purse I set out and I'm indignant as they slam out the door. Their loud voices and poor departure etiquette are something that could've easily awakened the baby. This incident is definitely something to be reported to hotel management. They must be reprimanded.

Chapter 20

THE MOMENT OF RUTH

I'm waiting for Ruth by this absolutely spectacular creek and she's late. Or maybe I'm early? But I remember how she was never on time when we worked together at the hair salon in college. I sit with the stroller lodged against some rocks and look around. It truly is exquisite here and makes me think about the time I went river-rafting in California and fell out into the turbulent rapids. I still have the scrapes to prove my dare-devil behavior.

Is that her? There's a figure dressed in bright red with long blonde hair about a quarter mile away. But that can't be her because this person is clinging to a very tall male dressed in white. I'm quite positive Sam wasn't coming today but if he did, he didn't suddenly grow several inches in height.

The two people part ways after a few more minutes of cozy embracing. The red woman walks in my direction. Soon she waves to me. I can't believe that she's motioned to me and I stand stupidly, afraid to return the gesture. She obviously takes me for someone else.

But when the person gets a little closer, I see it is indeed Ruth. She breaks into a light jog to reach me and gives a little hug. I smell her familiar shampoo, Flex, she used to use it in high school. I also smell men's cologne. She's wearing red Capri's and a red dancer's type top, the kind that exposes her slender upper arms.

I struggle to maneuver the stroller out of the rocks that hem it in.

"Oh, I forgot to tell you to wear Ava Rose in one of those front pack cuddlers. The rocks here can be a bitch. I left Caden at home with our nanny for that very reason. Let's walk over on that cleared path instead," Ruth says, pointing.

As we walk, I'm prepared for Ruth's next question.

"Wow, how did your eye heal so fast?"

"Thank god for make-up," I say. "Can you imagine walking around with a shiner like that?"

She nods. "Oh my god, I'd be lost without it some mornings. I especially give thanks for the person that invented waterproof mascara. I love looking beautiful when I cry."

When we reach the trail, Ruth turns to me with a tremendous amount of seriousness. I feel that sudden trepidation again. Nathan has called her back. I just know it.

"I'm lying. Lying and cheating," Ruth tells me. "C'mon, let's walk this way."

I'm stunned. "For how long?" I manage to ask.

"For an hour maybe. Unless we get tired before."

"No, the affair. How long have you been having it?" I persist.

"Oh! Just a few weeks. It's very new. You picked an exciting time to visit me, my dear."

"You're going to leave Sam?"

"No. Well, maybe. Eventually. Right now this is just good, wild sex. You wouldn't believe some of the positions we've tried. But I'm going to end it soon. I'm giving myself two more weeks to indulge," she states unabashedly. "Then I go back to real life. You know what? Let's scrap this and head to my house. I'm starved. Do you mind?"

I think about what Ruth says and feel a little envious. She desires good, wild sex so she finds it. She's starved and so she feeds herself.

Ruth's home looks far different in the daylight than it did the evening before. Gaudy and glitzy. That's another reason I prefer darker to sunnier, even flashy things don't look quite as garish on cloudy days. I meet Caden for the first time as the Mexican housekeeper carries him out gingerly. He's pretty small in size but Ruth remarks that he's seeing a specialist for mild growth problems. He's the spitting image of Sam, and I'm glad her husband doesn't have reason to question his paternity.

Ruth hands the housekeeper, who is introduced as Rosa, a nearby camera and asks the maid to take a photograph of us holding our babies. I try to recall if I've ever told Ruth my feelings on how important pictures are. The flash causes me to blink.

We set each baby next to each other on a floor quilt and immediately both of us hold up rattles to shake at them while we continue conversing.

"So yes, Scott. I met him on one of those online affair sights for married people."

"There are organized places to cheat on the web?" I'm incredulous.

"Honey, there's a vast array of options. It's practically like a Chinese to-go menu," she jokes. I imagine ordering a 6 ft, curly-haired man holding a side of Won-Ton soup."

"It's called *RareAffair.com* and their motto is 'When monogamy becomes monotony'."

Suddenly I feel like this could be a trap. Ruth is confiding in me about her flaws in an effort to get me to do the same. Expressing your own vulnerability fosters intimacy, everyone knows that.

In the background, I observe the housekeeper swiping a black lacquer grand piano in the living room with a feather duster. It seems to me that just spreads the dirt around more evenly.

"I love what you've got her dressed in," Ruth changes the subject completely. I look at the polka-dotted pinafore dress and white pantaloons I also picked up at Laura Ashley and can't help but agree.

"I so wish I had a girl. I get so tired of boy's overalls," Ruth laments.

"Oh, I don't know. I'm already a little bored with all the lace and frills," I say to throw her off any track.

"But you have such choice and variety with a girl," says fashion plate Ruth. "If you're tired of girly, you can do the cute tom-boy thing. On the other hand with a boy, if you're bored with masculine, you can't suddenly put him in a dress. You'd be accused of raising a pansy or damaging him forever."

I think about leaving right now. This very instant. Leaving Ruth's house, leaving my hotel, and leaving Colorado. I don't like this immoral woman anymore and I don't know how we were ever best friends in high school. My expression must've looked ugly because Ruth tells me I seem stressed and suggests we go out to dinner. She volunteers her housekeeper as a babysitter and says Sam is working late so it's girl's night out. I tell her that I didn't bring anything nicer than the work-out clothes I'm currently wearing, but she insists I go upstairs to her closet and pick anything I like. It's awkward and I can't think of any way out of this scenario, so I head up the steps. I'll come up with a stomach problem in a half hour or so and beg off.

Upstairs, Ruth's room shows no sign of any male recently or ever residing in it. There are night tables draped with flounce-edged cream colored linen, cut crystal bowls, vases and display pedestals with oodles of jewels and liquid silver chains draped from them. Everything has her feminine touch. The furniture looks futuristic with its clear, acrylic fronts and I've never seen dressers and bureaus where the drawers are literally transparent, showing the clothing folded neatly inside. I'm grateful my messy chests are the old-fashioned kind, opaque and private.

Now I see where Sam is represented here. He has his own closet. His drawers stand unobtrusively inside the walk-in and all his jeans hang neatly there too. I run my hands through the hangers and don't see any evidence of even one suit. Strange for a professional. There's one lone bottle of cologne and a walnut wooden tray for holding loose change. His watches (he has five or six) sit atop the chest. And that's it.

The other closet must be Ruth's and the reason I make this guess is because it is substantially larger. She has her clothing both color and seasonally coordinated and all this organization makes me dizzy. I hear a noise from downstairs and poke my head out to shout.

"Everything okay down there?"

"Yes. That's just Caden getting fussy. Ava is a dream. So think about if you want Mexican or Thai food. Kay?" Ruth's voice floats up to me.

I hear a new tone. Higher pitched. Who is that?

"Senora, Puedo ir al doctor con mi hermana por apenas un poco rato por favor? Si?" I recognize the housekeeper, although she's muffled.

"Si, Si," acknowledges Ruth.

The front door opens and bangs shut. What follows is the unmistakable cry of my baby, no doubt from the slammed door. But I'm only half-dressed and Ruth's skirt is too tight and not zipping, of course. It makes me uneasy hearing him cry while I'm so far away. I can't comfort him. Yes, him. Oh my God. HIM!

"Ruth, I'm coming. Don't do anything at all. I'm coming," I say keeping my voice casual.

"Oh, Ava's wet. Just a quick diaper change," Ruth projects at full volume.

Terror grips my insides and my stomach muscles tense. "No!" but no voice comes out. I sit down on Ruth's velvet dressing stool, to steady my shaking. Calm down. She won't do it. She's just alerting me to come down and do it myself.

"I'll be right there, Ruth. She doesn't like unfamiliar hands," I say gaily, lips quivering involuntarily.

Silence. Why is there silence? As long as I can keep her talking, I know everything is fine.

Suddenly I think I hear a peculiar yelp, but it could be either of the babies. Or a dog. Was it a yip? Do they own a dog? It couldn't be Ruth's sickened expression, could it?

"Ruth, could you have a glass of water for me as soon as I come down?" I holler louder now. "I'm extremely parched. Right away, please." Anything to keep her busy. My mind races. There! Finally, my own clothes are back on and I take the carpeted stairs two at a time, almost slipping in my socks.

I round the corner, teeth chattering, to see Ruth's fingers on the buttons of my baby's pinafore dress.

"What are you doing?" I ask coldly.

"Oh," is her voice trembling? "I'm just admiring the detail on this dress. Expertly finished," she tells me without looking up, so engrossed is she. Did Ruth ever sew?

I notice she hasn't gotten me the water yet. So what has she been doing all this time? Ruth watches my face as I scan the room for anything that's different. Were the diapers always sitting out like that? The camera seems to have been moved. Wait, that's definitely different! Half-hidden under the sofa, a pair of white ruffled pantaloons stick out. And they're inside-out! Ruth follows my gaze and sees where it stops. Now we both turn to stare at one another.

"You undressed my baby. Didn't you?" I ask, measuring my words in staccato rhythm. I can see her pronounced swallow.

"Oh yeah, I started to change her diaper but then I thought no, no, no, that's a mommy's job," she says cutely. "So I stopped." But I notice her face twists and she looks like she's about to cry. Ruth then looks away but I can see rapid blinking from her side profile.

"You're lying. I don't trust you," I say from somewhere inside myself.

Ruth slinks toward the entry hallway. What is she moving toward? I follow.

"But that's just it, Nordie. You can trust me. With whatever is going on, honey."

I look hard at her and think for a moment. I remember her hilarity at my nonsensical joke the other night. She could have just been acting polite, I suppose. Behind me both babies start to whine but I keep my gaze firmly fixed on Ruth.

"Lots of women want daughters, Nordis. Even I want one," she continues merrily and ends with a stilted giggle.

"Well, you can't have mine!" I say with a threatening pitch that scares even me. Ruth shakes her head.

"No, no. Of course not." I recognize this soothing, restful tone from her now. I used it myself when I worked on the phone helpline. It irritates me.

"Let's just talk. Post-partum blues. They suck. I should know. After all, my affair is just . . ." but she seems to think better of that direction and changes course. "A good therapist with a good prescription can do wonders, believe me."

"No," I say and crouch down low on my knees, cradling my head deep in my hands. Everything is spinning. She'll tell Nathan. Or worse.

"Do you feel sick? I'll just call a doctor." I look up and realize she's been creeping toward her cell phone which sits on a pedestal, just one of many that exhibit all their valuable entryway art. Now she's boldly pushing buttons that beep loud and clear.

"You're calling child protective services," I accuse. "They'll take my baby." All at once, I leap and lunge forcefully at her with my intently outstretched arms.

"No, no. Gawd no," screeches Ruth and shields her face with her hands, but it's too late. Why does she guard her face like that? It's her head that needs protection. I realize I've knocked into the platform that displays the marble Michelangelo David statue and now the entire thing tips and comes crashing down. It bashes Ruth's head in straight from the top. After it gashes her skull, it falls to the floor with an alarming thwack. Behind me, the babies scream ear-piercing hysterics.

Ruth collapses in a heap and blood trickles from her head. Her cell phone completes the original call from the wooden floor. I can hear the internal ringing and then a click. "Good morning, Dr's office," the receptionist chirps. "Hello? Hello? Do you have a baby crying?" I reach over Ruth's still body and disconnect.

The last thing I remember seeing before I shut my own eyes are the large shards of granite carving scattered about on the maple floor and David's overt maleness, which is also on the ground—entirely and eerily intact.

Chapter 21

SEEING RED

When babies cry, most people will do anything to quiet them down. And normally that would be my first priority as well. However, sitting on the floor with my eyes squeezed shut, these two little ones howling at the same time takes me back to my days of having twin infants. And it's actually a peaceful and serene sound, their screams; the memory is heartwarming for me. The twins are hungry again I recall, better wake up Nathan so we can feed them together in our dual rocking chairs. I realize of course, that what I am doing is going back to a better place so I don't have to be here. Here is not good. But once you realize what you are doing and why, you can then choose to stop doing it.

I open my eyes and see the pool of blood widening around Ruth's head. That's a horrible, dreadful injury. But it's just an injury, I think woozily. I make comforting, shushing sounds toward the babies, who are red-faced and squirming behind me, then run upstairs calling out in my broken Spanish to make sure the housekeeper really did leave earlier. "Hola? Hola? Rosa Aqui? Usted Aqui?" There's nobody else in this house. I am alone. I'm not sure which pounds more, my heart or my head. And I don't know why I think to do what I do next. But this is what I do.

I race into Ruth's bedroom where I was just trying on clothes moments ago, this time I veer into Sam's stark closet. I grab the cologne and a wristwatch with a red face that caught my eye earlier and run back downstairs. I slide the red watch under Ruth's body and startle when I notice the digital numbers read 11:11. I spritz some of his scent onto her clothing. I dash back up that spiral staircase, wipe the cologne bottle with tissue and return it to its rightful place in Sam's closet.

As I dart out, my eye catches on an enormous wedding portrait mounted over their bed. It looks like a real artist's painting on canvas and not just some enlarged photo. The happy couple is posed in front of a most striking sunset; the sky is made up of individually streaked reddish hues. In junior high, Ruth and I used to describe our billowing, Cinderella style wedding gowns to one another. But her dress is form-fitting and severe in this masterpiece. Sam's eyes seem moist and kind. Forgiving?

I run downstairs, avert my gaze from Ruth, sling a baby over each of my shoulders and hasten to the driveway where I screech away from this entire thing as quickly as I can in my rental car.

I'm not aware of any of the drive except for hearing a siren and I wince and sing a loud lullaby to cover up its whimpering whine. Could they be coming for Ruth? Coming for me? Or could it just be the sound of the babies fussing and not a siren at all? But then I spy a police car pursuing another speeding vehicle and remind myself that law enforcement only chases bad people. Not people who just make mistakes, not people who know right from wrong. They don't go after that kind. The police can tell the difference between intent and accident.

Suddenly I'm in the lobby of my hotel and Audrey and the other front desk personnel are casting me unusual looks as I skulk by, carrying both sleeping babies. This is unusual. A very unusual situation. But it's going to be okay. It has to be okay. I never meant for anything like this to happen. I only meant to have a couple of weeks of contentment. Is that so much to want when you've just been cheated out of a lifetime of it? My tears dampen Caden's little red onesie.

My room grows even smaller and more claustrophobic with both babies settled inside. But in a few hours, Caden won't be here, I'm sure. Maybe I won't be here either. I freeze at the thought. What would happen to my baby if they haul me away? To my other children at home? Oh my god. The enormity of the situation filters in and I'm shuddering. I need to write home and let them all know I've made a terrible error and I'm coming back right away. I'll say they should expect me tomorrow morning and I'm ready to participate fully in my life now. I'm good to go. (I hate when people use that expression) I'll emphasize that I thought I needed a longer time away but the bonding has completed much sooner than I thought. Strong, powerful bonding. I even sleep with the baby now. They'll like hearing that and we'll all go out to dinner together, the kids, Nathan, my mom and me to celebrate. It's not too late.

I log into my email on the hotel computer to quickly write the letter I've just composed in my head. To undo everything. Things can be put back the way they were. It isn't too late. It's never too late, my Jewish grandmother used to tell me. After I click "send" I'll pack up, check-out and be on my way. I might even arrive home before they read this email and then won't they be surprised! But it takes an extremely long time to connect to the internet and while it flashes an annoying red hourglass at me, I think just to be on the safe side, I should dye my hair a deep brown. That way if anyone is looking for anyone, (and I'm sure they won't be) but if anyone happens to be searching, it will be for a red-haired woman with a baby girl named Ava Rose and not a brunette lady with a baby boy called Charlie.

Ruth is only injured, I tell myself. A small amount of blood that a few stitches will certainly take care of. Rosa will come home and know what to do. She'll call Sam because housekeepers always call their bosses. They don't like to mess with the police. Besides, Sam is a surgeon, right? He'll rush right home and fix her up right there in the house with his doctor kit. Good as new. The whole thing will go unreported to any official agency.

As I'm thinking this through a bit more thoroughly, my internet homepage snaps open and I'm astounded to see the list of emails I've received in my inbox. It looks like every person I've ever known in my lifetime (Nathan must've called them all on the phone) has written to me in the past two days. And many subject titles are in all caps and urgent looking with two or three exclamation marks. There are five alone sent just from my mother, three from Brenna and one, two, three, oh my God, there are eight emails from Nathan. I'm colder now than ever. Boulder is really a chilling, hostile environment and I pull my turtleneck sweater up over my chin.

The jackhammer knock at the door has startled the babies (not to mention me) and now they're starting to screech again. It's probably the hotel manager with a crib that has become available. I can tell him we won't need it anymore. We're checking out immediately and that will save time downstairs in the lobby. I hurry to open it before the loud pounding starts up again.

Two police officers tower before me, each flashing their badges in bright red cases. They identify themselves, identify me and ask if I know a Ruthany Manning? My eyes look really surprised and I nod yes and tell them I'm with her son right now, babysitting. I open the door a little wider so they can see this is true.

"Is everything alright?" I ask. I have a strong urge to check on the lump in my left breast right now but I can't do that with them watching me.

"Her housekeeper said you were at her house visiting with her earlier today?"

"Yes, we walked together and then we came back to her home and talked. After that she asked me if I could watch her son for a while, since our little ones are the same age. She needed to do something personal. Is everything alright?"

"Mrs. Manning is in the hospital, listed in critical condition with a head injury, possibly a coma. You were the last one to be seen with her, according to the Manning maid who found her on the floor."

My whole body starts quavering but I simultaneously shake my head so vehemently, it looks like the source of all the movement originates from my adamant "No!"

"Oh no!" I say. "When I left Ruth, she was completely fine. What happened? In fact she was rehearsing what she was going to say to her husband. She wanted to tell him she was having an affair. And that she was leaving him." I pause so I don't speed-talk this thing. "She was really worried about his reaction and that's why she asked me to babysit." I'm still shaking my head back and forth in that "no" position so forcefully that I see strands of red curls cross into my peripheral vision.

Chapter 22

SEAL THE DEAL

I shoplifted once, when I was in college. I won't blame it on the antidepressant medication I was on at the time, although I think that had something to do with it. It was a foolish, young adult type of impulsiveness really—a sparkly belt from an exclusive dress shop called "Fuji Fashion and Couture" which I casually tried to wear out to the parking lot underneath my coat. (It was one of those hot, sunny days when I was feeling fat, so wearing a jacket in weather like that probably added to the suspiciousness of the scenario.) When the overhead door alarm buzzed obnoxiously, I whipped my head around from left to right, as if I had no clue why such a thing would happen.

After patting me down, the haughty female manager just sneered as I dopily attempted my excuse. I elaborated on how I was taking a medication that made me groggy and confused, even careless. I offered proof by pulling the prescription vial out from my purse. She showed her sympathy by squeezing my arm painfully tight and shouting for the shop owner, a short Asian gentleman who proceeded to demand my driver's license. Customers turned to stare at me.

"This is a mistake. I didn't realize I still had the belt on," I said. "I'm out of it. The side-effects from medicine. Confusion. Don't you understand the difference between accident and on purpose?" I asked indignantly.

"Nordis Spect," he read sharply, holding my license close to his eyes. "No respect!" I never realized my name sounded like that to others. I started to feel a little afraid. These people weren't even remotely close to apologizing for ridiculing me in public.

He spoke in angry, rapid-fire Japanese to the smug female manager, who I thought couldn't possibly understand a word, but then she translated aloud with a smirk.

"He says he should call the cops but he won't. He says there's not enough shame in your society. He wants to shame you. He'll call your husband." I fought back tears because innocent people shouldn't cry.

"But I'm not married," I said. I was engaged at the time.

The manager reiterated back to the owner what I said. He furiously held the belt high up in the air. I'll never forget his words.

"Anata Otousan."

"Your father," the manager taunted.

"Oh, please don't call my father," I wept openly now as the store owner picked up an oversized Polaroid camera and clicked it to flash straight in my face, my eyes temporarily blinded.

It wasn't that I feared my father's punishment, physical beating or grounding because obviously I was beyond all that in my years, even though I still lived at home. I simply dreaded the sad, poignant look that would come into his eyes each and every time I was in his presence. It was something I'd experienced once before for a far milder transgression. And it wasn't something I could ever bear again.

My father was a holocaust survivor and only wanted our utmost success and happiness. I would rather deal with the police and be arrested, so terrified was I of my father's own particular brand of disappointment and disapproval. Right then and there in the dress shop, I struck an internal bargain with myself and sealed it with my silent, solemn promise. "I promise to talk directly with the police if my father is allowed to stay blissfully unaware of all this. Please."

But something in my demeanor must've swayed the quick-tempered shop owner because without warning he shouted in staccato beats of English.

"You go now. Now you go!"

I fled the building, never looking back. Ruth later told me that during a subsequent shopping excursion with her mother, she had seen my photograph displayed prominently near the cash register with a sign, "No Respect, No Shame." I swore her to secrecy and explained the deal I made that day with myself; how I'd talk to the police if only my father would never have to know what his daughter did. Ruth assured me that she understood.

Apparently the day has come for me to keep my part of the deal and so I face the officers squarely and realize that one of them has been speaking all this time. I only hear the ending.

". . . child protective services for your daughter while you're taken in for questioning."

"Oh my god, no!" I say. "This is a nursing baby. Please, I've done nothing wrong and neither has she." It crosses my mind they could ask me to breastfeed right now as proof, but that would be absurd.

The two police officers exchange glances and I can tell that, like the Asian store owner all those years ago, something in my plea impacts them. They call for assistance with Caden (I feel terrible about separating from him too, but at least he isn't dressed like a girl) and after he's safely in the arms of a female officer, they escort me and the baby into their patrol car.

When we arrive at the station house, I clutch my baby protectively to my chest as they lead me through back rooms. All eyes seem to be on me and my face feels flushed. They have me peer through a one way window to identify Sam who literally sits three feet away on the other side of the wall. Sam.

He slumps motionless, head down, a hand covering his forehead. I analyze this hand and the fingers, and the wrist. It's an oversized, burly hand, the kind that would engulf a child's, with its strong fingers and a wide diameter wrist bone; possibly capable of flinging someone to the ground, or a hard, swift blow to the head if angered. Is Sam angry? No, Sam is sad. Very sad. I can tell this immediately when, upon direction of the interior officer, he slowly lifts his head as if it's weighted and stares intently through the window with a faraway look on his face. Can Sam see me? He gazes directly my way with these soft, luminous, moist eyes. Those are the eyes from the wedding portrait.

After the positive identification is made, I sit and answer very easy questions. I have primed for all these questions. I am even able to tell them the first name of Ruth's lover. I remember she told me Scott. I tell them exactly how Ruth met Scott and I'm even able to recall the specific name of the internet affair site and I describe the clothing he wore at Boulder Creek. I talk about my friendship with Ruth and how we used to tell each other everything in high school and how easy it was to pick up right where we left off. Yes, Ruth confided in me. I knew her long term plans and they did not include Sam.

Next, a question about carseats. Carseats? I ask for a repeat of the question, to buy time and for clarification purposes. My mind rummages through memories. What could a carseat have to do with any of this? Finally it becomes painfully clear. Evidently Sam has insisted Ruth would never ever permit me to take baby Caden out of the house without his infant carseat. And his carseat remains exactly as always; right smack in the middle of the backseat in their Lexus. The questioning officer leans forward for my response. So do the others.

I will myself to focus on what seems to be a very significant issue to everyone here. My breast lump is bothering me but the carseat mystery must be adequately explained. But how? I remember that in my rush to leave Ruth's house, I gently laid both babies on the back seat floor, cuddled in warm blankets. I knew I hadn't far to drive and I simply couldn't risk the time. But if things had been leisurely and as a diligent mother, of course I would've strapped both babies into carseats. And yes! I could've done so, I suddenly brighten, as it comes back to me that I tossed a spare one in the trunk of the rental car. "This one is much prettier than ours," I remember saying to the female rental clerk. That's it—that's the answer.

Hoping I don't leave too much space between the officer's question and my response, I plunge ahead. "Oh, no worries. (I hate when people say that,) I didn't need the Manning's carseat because I actually had two of my own, one for each baby. The rental car came with one and I had taken ours from home for the plane ride. Shall I go get them?" I ask cooperatively. I wish I didn't add that last part. It sounds too eager.

The officer looks at his watch, scribbles some notes and requests that yes, I should fetch both seats. I'm keen on getting out of there with my baby until I realize that I don't get to go alone. They are having someone, a Detective Kern, accompany me "home." If only I really could go home, I sigh and think of my other children. Suddenly another panicky feeling spreads through my insides. If Detective Kern comes with me, he will see the carseat in the trunk and not the back seat. He will deduce that Caden has never used it.

I ask if I can go to the restroom and they point the way. I wonder if they will have someone accompany me there too, but they do not. I truly have to pee, but I'm also hoping if I take long enough, they'll decide it's getting late and forego this hunting expedition.

The bathroom is disgustingly filthy and there's no place to set my baby down even for a second. I guess there's not a heavy demand for a changing table at a police station. As I survey the situation, the door hinges whoosh and in blows a distraught woman, seemingly my age—makeup streaked and clothing mismatched, she evidently had been urgently roused from sleep to come here. Even in her disarrayed state, she politely offers to hold my baby so I can use the facilities. I hesitate. I will not risk anyone else probing into my baby's diaper, but she reaches her arms out kindly and I deem it safe for two seconds.

As I lock the door and rush through the motions, the woman carries on a conversation by herself, her words floating over the stall to me.

My boy. My Van. It's his second domestic violence arrest with his girlfriend. He lost his job at the hotel. It's his temper. He's got his father's temper. Be grateful you have a sweet little girl." I hear clucking and cooing sounds.

When I come out, she is still captivated with the baby and I take the opportunity after observing her mussed face, to at least smooth my own wild hair. The countertop is soiled with blood droplets and it turns my stomach. I set my diaper bag down in the only halfway clean spot—inside the sink.

I keep my eye on the mirrored reflection of the woman hugging my baby as I run a trembling hand over my hair. Suddenly the lady makes surprised sounds, pointing and gesturing frantically, which makes me more nervous. But I turn to see she's motioning toward the sink where my oversized purse has set off the automatic sensor and water spurts into my leather bag, setting its contents afloat.

I sheepishly retrieve my baby, wish the woman well and head back toward the conference room with my dripping diaper bag. Instead of immediately entering, I loiter outside the door momentarily to listen in.

". . . if you just found out some guy was screwing your wife and now she's leaving you for him," the officer says.

"Yeah, and I still say she's your typical stay-at-home mom type. Baby-sits and probably knits blankets."

"Okay then, just check the carseats and she's out. Get the maid back in here."

"She legal?"

"Who knows, run her info. Hey, you on the Bronson case, man? I just called and . . ."

But an official looking woman swiftly strides down the hallway so I pretend to rummage inside my purse and pull out a soggy tissue. She gives me a peculiar look as she passes. When I walk in, there are nods all around from the officers as they stand at my presence. It almost seems like an opportune time to tell my mustard joke, but I think better of that and instead find myself following a detective to his patrol car, holding my baby and hoping for the best.

It's after midnight and I feign sleep in the back of the squad car, my chin resting against the baby's smooth velvety head. I'm acutely tuned-in to the front seat and I can tell this Detective Kern is in charge here or at least he's someone quite important. He confers with a steady stream of droning radio voices as we veer through the dark, cold, starless night.

In the hotel parking lot, I direct him to where my car is parked. Suddenly a clicking signal comes over the short-wave radio, and Detective Kern picks it up to listen directly, hunching down in his seat for a private conversation. I take this opportunity of distraction to discreetly hop out and quickly pop the trunk of my car to obtain the carseat in question. Please, I think, don't let him watch me. A moment later, as I tiptoe up behind him with both carseats, I overhear him on the radio asking for the time of death and then he abruptly signs off.

"Oh," he looks at me bemused. "Why did you bother pulling them out from your backseat?" I start to sweat and can feel my breast lump growing in size.

"I just needed to visually verify there are two." Detective Kern looks at both seats and then intently at me and my sleeping baby.

"She's cute," he says. "My wife is pregnant with our first and we really want a girl. After seeing all the boys down in Juvi Hall, I don't want to deal with that," he finishes. I nod and force what I hope looks like a laid-back yawn.

"Okay," he says kindly but keeps staring oddly. "Well, I guess it's late. Your story checks. You're clear." Should I give him a grateful smile? As I try and decide, Detective Kern continues, "I'm sorry to have to tell you this, Ms. Spect, but you may not leave town until further notice. You're our only material witness in this murder case. Tonight at 11:11 pm, Ruthany Manning died."

Chapter 23

CONNECTING THE DOTS

Upstairs in the hotel room, I finally collapse on the bed and allow myself to tremble and cry. The baby makes excellent eye contact nowadays and he focuses intently on me with his emerald greens until his little eyes cross involuntarily. As the sobs reverberate, I know a little baby shouldn't see his mother weeping like this and so I force myself to stop.

I think about Ruth who wanted to look beautiful while crying. What would she have wanted to look like dying? I can't let myself begin to think this way, but somewhere in the universe, a tiny thought has formulated and transforms itself into the shape of a question. It flits and floats, like the marabou fluff in our mother-daughter portrait, wafting through the air, drifting down, down, faster and faster now, until it finds the perfect place to alight—deep inside the recesses of my consciousness. Gently I pluck this question, pondering its appearance from every angle, grappling its weight and gradually it begs to be asked.

What is the difference between involuntary manslaughter and first degree murder?

But what kind of person even contemplates such a question? I am finished with all this. Detective Kern even told me so. I am clear. In the clear. So that means I am done. At the end of the day (I really hate that expression) that's all that matters. My contacts bother me.

The thought of calling Nathan now, as I planned earlier, is utterly exhausting. I can't even imagine his questions, let alone my answers. Instead I want to call Brenna. It won't be the first time I've called her this late at night. She and I had our best conversations in the wee hours those first few weeks after we gave birth. We shared secret details by phone while she nursed and I gave a bottle. One time we even stayed up the entire night talking, kindred spirits with kindled sparks catching ablaze. Tonight I need that friendship flame more than ever, a warm fire of intimacy, blanketing a cold and scary night for me.

"Nordis?" Brenna answers the phone on the first ring. How does she know it's me? But then I realize it is the lateness of the hour. Of course it would be me.

"Brenna, I can't tell you where I am but I'm doing okay and really this has been a much needed thing for . . ." Brenna cuts me off.

"Nordis," she says, not bothering to hide her urgency. "I was at your home last night. Nathan asked me to come over to answer some questions. The way he was looking at me, I can tell he doesn't believe me. He wants to know everything you've confided in me since we've met and I don't know how long I can put him off. Last night I told him I couldn't stay long because Bridget was sick, and she is Nordis, she's very sick, but there's . . ."

"I'm so sorry, Brenna," I interrupt as I touch my breast lump and it's harder now.

"Nordis, there's something else. When I was inside your house last night, I looked around and saw lots of family pictures framed on your fireplace mantle."

"Yes?" I ask, wondering if she also has a special fondness for photographs like I do.

"There's a picture of you, your husband and an older woman with twin boys on the beach?" She pauses.

"Mmm," I say, knowing exactly the photo she means. It was taken on the twin's third birthday in Laguna Beach.

"I recognize the older woman in the photo, Nordis. That's the same woman I told you came by our house at the end of my pregnancy to talk to my mother about adopting my baby."

I freeze, holding the receiver tightly to my ear. The woman in the photo is my mother.

Chapter 24

Dream Extreme

Brenna and I talk late into the night and when I fall asleep my dreams keep me in a constant state of agitation and trickling sweat. First the marble David statue in Ruth's house has the ability to speak. He gives an interview to Detective Kern describing exactly what he saw happen. Afterwards, Detective Kern announces on his radio that Nordis Spect has no respect. I wake up, heart racing and breathless only to fall back asleep and slip into the next continuous nightmare, equally as vivid.

Sam is jailed and starving, I dream. His body has dwindled to nothing and the only thing left are his eyes and hands which he implores me to take away when I visit him behind bars. Tears from his eyeballs overflow his palms and the whole situation is awkward and messy for me. I leave, promising to care for his body parts but then bump into my mother on the street. My mother is wearing a dress exactly like mine. We look like twins. She asks passersby if they can tell us apart? "Bet you can't tell who the mother is and who is the daughter," she goads flirtatiously to men who walk by and gape. Suddenly she spins around, twirling faster and faster—a hazy blur, and when she stops, baby Bridget is in her arms. Nathan comes around the corner and greets her as his wife. The three of them walk off leaving me holding Sam's eyes and hands which I stuff inside my drenched purse.

I startle awake, unable to catch my breath. I seek out the clock. The baby sleeps peacefully and beyond him, I can see the glow of the digital numerals shining 3:30 am. In twelve hours Brenna will be here and I will pick her up at the airport. I use the remote to turn on the television but quickly employ the mute button. There is that smiling local anchor woman I've come to know named Paulette. Her jovial face turns somber as the words appear below across the screen. "Prominent Local Breast Surgeon Suspect in Wife's Murder." Now her mouth moves quickly but still silently because my finger is paralyzed over the remote. There's the front of Ruth's house and there is Sam. He stands alone and forlorn, tightening his jacket but his eyes and hands seem okay to me. By the time I un-mute the sound, there's only four words left to hear in the story.

". . . in a jealous rage." Then it's on to Boulder's forecast which is slated for snow, the meteorologist cheerily reports. I certainly hope Brenna's flight will not be canceled due to inclement weather.

Last night Brenna and I decided since I cannot leave town, she and Bridget will come to Colorado. She will not tell her parents where she is going and I'll pay for her airfare. I can't even begin to make sense of what she has told me. In the hospital when we had the first of many chats, she relayed to me how upset and disappointed her mother, Barbara, felt at her daughter's pregnancy, particularly at such a tender age. Barbara tried to talk her into an abortion, reminding her of her dancing career. But Brenna wouldn't even entertain the idea for a single minute.

When the time for ending the pregnancy had elapsed, without consulting Brenna, Barbara had spoken to Dr. Grant (who also works with infertile couples) in the hopes he could make a connection and the baby would be placed with a nice couple at birth. I think back to how upset Brenna had been telling me this story, but then we were interrupted for a "How to bathe your newborn" lesson.

Another time in the new mother's lounge, as we waited together for the nurses to bring us more diapers, Brenna elaborated about one strange night in her last trimester. An older woman, dressed young and hip but who seemed very nervous, came over to try and convince Brenna to let her adopt the baby. Brenna said she disliked the woman immediately when the woman pressured Brenna to find out what sex the child was. Barbara badgered her young daughter to consider an adoption with this woman, offering to whisk Brenna off to Europe for an exotic vacation and a brand new, post-pregnancy designer wardrobe if she did so, stressing that she could also get back to her dancing goals.

Brenna reported that this elderly looking woman said she was infertile and her husband was an important doctor who performed rare surgeries and was traveling out of the country at the moment. The talk was disturbing to Brenna and she made it clear in front of both women that she would, in no uncertain terms, not give up her baby. Apparently this woman and Barbara hit it off and Brenna watched tearfully as they traded contact information to touch base in the future. As the woman departed, she received a phone call that Brenna was certain was from, if not her supposed husband, a male caller. The last thing Brenna reported overhearing this woman say before she left was, "Youth is wasted on the young."

As I think about this conversation, I berate myself for not recognizing back then that this was my mother. After all, that asinine quote is something only she would recite. But now I sit here incredulous at all the potential ramifications. Why on earth would my mother want to adopt a baby? Who was the male voice on the phone? There must be some possible mistake because there can be no plausible explanation.

My hotel phone rings but nobody, not even Brenna, knows I am staying here. In fact the only person that has called me at this number before was Ruth and she . . . well she can't do that anymore. I answer and prepare to tell the caller they have the wrong room. I'm shocked to hear it is Sam on the other end of the line. He tells me he is using Ruth's cell phone to reach me. There is silence between us for a moment when he awkwardly informs me he's been released on bail and asks if I can come to his home? As the last person who saw Ruth alive, he has a few questions for me.

As I hang up, I wonder why he thinks I would even consider coming alone to the house to see a suspected killer. But then it dawns on me—he must know some good reason why I am not frightened of him.

Chapter 25

TO UNHINGE A BINGE

When you binge, you are out of control. But if you plan a binge in advance, does that put you in charge again? Some people go on shopping binges—you might think I did that recently with all the baby clothes I purchased—but I just call that a planned shopping spree. Some people fly to Las Vegas, intending to amuse themselves in the casino, when suddenly they're staying up all hours of the night, losing money they don't have and homes they really need. That's definitely taking entertainment overboard. People have sexual binges and I imagine it involves more than just the addiction to orgasm because they could achieve that all on their own. Alcohol and drug binges are self-explanatory, and we have plenty of support groups dedicated to help individuals who fall off those wagons. It's all about moderation. Just do something a little bit, and you're okay. You're good to go. (I really don't like that expression) Or if you can't be moderate, then don't do it at all. Avoid the temptation completely and that solves the problem too. End of story. We can live without shopping, gambling, drugs, sex and liquor.

But we cannot live without food.

Hotel room service must be accustomed to lots of strange requests because the two room stewards didn't bat an eye when they brought me up the romantic prime-rib dinner special for two that I ordered for lunch a few minutes ago. For lunch! Who orders this kind of heavy food for a mid-day meal? A salad is reasonable, even a sandwich is permissible but a five course gourmet feast before six o'clock can only mean one thing. And they knew it. And I knew they knew it.

"But where is her date? Could they have gotten in a lover's spat and he'll be back soon? Will all that decadence go to waste? Can a baby gum a baked potato?" All reasonable questions when you see a five foot, six inch, medium framed, red-headed woman alone in a room with a linen covered, candle-lit, rolling cart that's laden with calories, carbohydrates and cholesterol.

Everything is in place. The stewards are tipped, the door is closed, the shades are drawn, the lids are lifted and the mouth is gaping. Go!

Fast. That's how you must do it. Everything is inhaled without tasting it. If you slow down enough to enjoy it, you'll slow down enough to think. And that will be the end. Guzzle down the broccoli cheddar soup, the piping hot creaminess clogs your throat. No time to mash butter on the baked potato, just gulp the butter and sour cream straight from the condiment dish. Rip into the marbled meat and swig down the au jus sauce. The cheesecake can be devoured as its name suggests, just like a hunk of cheese. Ignore the heavy, rich, moist velvety texture. Silverware impedes the plan. The plan hinges on haste. Lingering invites guilt. You must fill the hollow with food so there's room for nothing else. Wait! Were those footsteps from the hall? Be ready to throw a bedspread over the whole thing if you're interrupted. But no, the deadbolt is locked. You are safe. You are not safe. You are alone with food.

My stomach lurches and I check the baby. Sleeping. This is good because babies cannot remember what they don't see. And if there are no witnesses, it didn't really happen. And even if there's some recall on my part, that's what tomorrow is for. And the day after. It's all about checks and balances. All or nothing. Even Steven. Pay the piper. Feast or famine. Push and pull. Up and down. Yin and yang. Black and white. In and out. What you put in, you must get out. This is the supreme form of balance.

Oh, I know. You think I'm going to make myself vomit, don't you? Of course you do. You've been talking to my mother, I'm sure. And it doesn't matter that I've already explained that my mother is prone to embellish details for effect. You think if even one tenth of what she said is true, then I must've been pretty bad off back then. Well, let's just think back on what the therapist said about it, shall we? The therapist's official report was that I had "disordered eating." That is not the same as an eating disorder. I was not an anorexic. I was not a bulimic. Disordered eating just means someone is prone to restricting and dieting, and once in a while under stress, a little bingeing. Well, of course I am all of that. I lost half my body weight eating only protein and vegetables for a year for goodness sake. What do you think that does to a person? Do you think I'm going to let all that effort go downhill just because I feel overwhelmed? All that discipline should go to waste? Or waist? All that hard work. And we haven't even delved into the exercising. The jogging. The racing. The sprinting. Do I strike you as someone who enjoys the outdoors and nature? Rising at the crack of dawn to enjoy a glorious, warm sunrise? Vigilant maintenance. That's what this kind of diligence is called. You slip up one time baby, and you'll be right back to square one. Or 240 pounds.

Here's how it works. It's easy and even though there's numbers involved, you can flunk out of algebra like I did and still make it work. Whatever weight I've gained tonight, let's be generous and say the scale in the hotel gym spits out a new number that's plus six pounds tomorrow. Okay, that's doable. That's probably only, let's say, a thirty-six hour fast. A complete fast. And just like the word implies, the time will go by "fast." You'll see. In fact, I have eaten so much these past fifteen minutes that I won't even feel one hunger pang. No room for hunger pangs, or any kind of pangs. No pangs of guilt allowed. Six pounds gained, six pounds lost. It's pure math. And if I'm not back to my initial weight after that, I'm certain that it's just another twelve hours of fasting to go. And don't forget the water. Water is the saving grace. Water is the cleanse of life. Drink it in and savor its purity. Water will flush out everything—all the poisons, toxins and contaminants. Then wash your hands with it. You're back in charge.

Chapter 26

THE PROZAC PRELUDE

I don't have nearly the food hangover that I've had during past eating frenzies, which is a good thing. My eyes are puffy and that's not a good thing so I take out the two room service spoons that I had placed in the mini-bar—just in case. I flinch as their icy cool metal touches my sensitive under eye skin. Sam and I have agreed that I will come by later this afternoon to talk. I shouldn't have picked today to binge. But I didn't pick today—it picked me.

I think about canceling. Surely Sam will understand a sick and cranky baby because he has one of his own. I get a retching feeling in my stomach when I think of Caden. Where is he? What do they do with little ones in cases like this? I look at my own baby and think of custody, wards of the state, foster care systems and . . . I must have had a scary expression because he screws up his tiny face and starts to wail pitifully. I pick him up and rub little circles on his back. I've frightened him. I've terrified myself.

I can't cancel anything because it will look too suspicious. I'm sure I can pull myself together and still have enough time to pick Brenna up from her plane. She won't mind watching both babies after I've paid for her flight. I will need some time to work on myself, some sit-ups and perhaps meditate or do self-relaxation exercises (which I used to think was hogwash but lately am finding a definite use for) because I know I cannot go back into Ruth's house without my breathing changing rhythm. And it will be noticeable. I know my pulse will quicken and my body will flush and I will start to have an anxiety attack. Perhaps my mother has a point about sometimes using medication for select situations.

But then I think back to a time when I was on Prozac. It was during my first marriage when my husband began complaining I wasn't as fun as I used to be when we were engaged. All the activities we used to enjoy together no longer brought me any pleasure and slowly, one by one, I eliminated them from my life. We no longer went river-rafting, played tennis together or traveled (after 911, I became fearful of flying) and even our marathon Scrabble games late into the night had been discarded. All I wanted to do was write and extensive, descriptive prose poured from pen to paper. All of it far too right-brained and abstract for a mechanical engineer to appreciate. Besides, my stories made him too morbid, he said.

One morning he reminded me that I was like this after the birth of our son as well and how stubborn I had been, refusing to seek help. It had almost cost us our marriage, he chastised. That night he came home with a prescription for antidepressants, telling me our relationship was once again in grave jeopardy and implored me to take them. They were prescribed by his engineering company's psychiatrist, Dr. Harlow. I had met her many times at office parties, fundraisers and holiday balls so I trusted her.

Two weeks after taking the green and white capsules, my mind felt muffled and foggy. I began having memory lapses and angry outbursts with friends and family. My creative energy dissipated and not only could I not conclude my writing in a profound manner, I couldn't even come up with an opening sparkly sentence. I became humorless too, finding worrisome warnings in people's puns and comical tales. But the biggest side effect was that I felt a sudden and heightened awareness of my body. The way I breathed, the way I walked, the way I chewed and even the way I sounded when I talked. My voice seemed suddenly too high pitched and shrill.

Don't stop taking the Prozac, that's the worst thing you can do, I kept hearing. This is just a temporary adjustment period so stick it out. Meanwhile, I was such a foreigner in my own body, it was all I could do to take care of my nine year old son. Hopeful that I would quickly rebound, my husband had rescheduled all our previous activities. As I sat on the sofa with a blank expression, I told him to find another tennis partner, go on an impending river-rafting trip without me, and waved him off in a tuxedo to his company holiday ball alone that year.

The only thing that interested me was an upcoming creative writing conference slated for one weekend in Las Vegas. Thrilled that I was showing enthusiasm for something, and hopeful that I had conquered my fear of flying, my well-intentioned spouse booked me a plane ticket and a hotel room in the nicest place on the strip—*the Mirage*. My mother begged to have my son for the weekend and my husband said he needed to catch up on some documentation work so I didn't feel too guilty leaving. Besides, maybe this really was the beginning of the depression lifting.

During the drive to the airport I pictured how thrilling it would be to meet the keynote speaker, Danielle Steel. For an extra grand, I was even going to have the opportunity to have her critique something I wrote. At that point, I realized I had forgotten to pack my Prozac. Frustrated that the very thing that might make me miss my trip was the very thing that would help me enjoy my trip, I turned the car around. If I hurried I could still make my flight.

I walked in our front door to the sight of strewn suitcases in the entry hall but there was no time for me to investigate. Perhaps my husband had a last minute business trip, I surmised. The Prozac bottle wasn't where I thought I left it in the kitchen so I took the stairs two at a time to hunt in the bedroom. Please, don't let it be lost now, I prayed, cursing my non-existent organizational skills.

When I opened the door, I realized that I needn't have worried—a new prescription could've easily been written for me right then and there. Just as soon as Dr. Harlow finished writhing, moaning and provocatively throwing her hair back as she straddled naked atop my soon-to-be ex-husband.

Chapter 27

THE NAKED TRUTH

Disembarking the plane, Brenna looks more like a frightened child than a capable mother and when I look into the baby carrier and see baby Bridget, I know why. As healthy, robust, and vigorous as my baby looks, hers is scrawny, limp and pale. It's all I can do to suppress a gasp. When they were born, they were virtually the same weight and height and now, at just over three weeks, mine looks his age but hers would definitely be classified as failing to thrive. Something compels me to reach out to this little one and when I do, she stretches slowly for my finger but can't quite coordinate her grasp because her fists stay tightly clenched. The slight movement is so strenuous for her that she lapses into sleep. I don't know what to say to Brenna.

"Oh. She's so tiny. What do the doctors say?" I manage.

"My father lost his job and we're only able to take her to this one public clinic. They've run all kinds of tests but so far they're not telling me anything," Brenna's voice wavers.

I give Brenna a hug and tell her that while she's here, we'll have Bridget seen by a specialist. I'm thinking of the doctor that Ruth mentioned who treated Caden.

"Actually, last night when I talked about our money problems to your husband, he said he'd send me to a doctor friend of his. He even offered to pay which I thought was so nice," Brenna tells me. That's so like Nathan, I think, helping out the underdog.

Brenna and I chatter a mile a minute and once again I can't help but feel extremely close with her, perhaps even motherly. She could be the teenage daughter that I should've had if my firstborn had been a girl. After all, they're around the same age. Lots of people have always told me to fulfill my need for a daughter by joining a Big Sister organization. Somehow that wouldn't be the same, yet keeping company with Brenna is extremely gratifying for me.

We get her and our babies settled into my room. I've already taken care to carefully hide all the girly clothing and my baby is wearing a simple yellow fleece suit that is appropriate for either a boy or a girl. Someday I'll confide in Brenna about my two week extravagance here, but now that seems to pale in comparison, in light of what's happened. I ask for the babysitting favor and she readily agrees. We plan on reconvening here in one hour and then we'll get to the bottom of what could be going on with my mother and possibly hers. As I leave, I notice that she lies down, probably planning on dozing while both babies also nap.

Outside I observe that it never did snow and in fact it's turned into an unusually sunny day for Colorado. I'm already overly warm in my light jacket and I nudge my sunglasses back up on my nose. I'm thinking of keeping them on indoors because the brightness will justify wearing them. It will be easier for me being around Sam with dark glasses on.

Before I knock on the Manning door, I purposely slow myself down. Moving, talking and even breathing fast are all signs of nervousness. I decide on ringing instead of rapping because that seems more refined.

When Sam opens the door, I'm taken aback by what I see and my respiration quickens once again. He's wildly unshaven, there's dried up tears on his scruffy cheeks, (which is to be expected) but he seems to have lost weight (in such a short amount of time?) and the spark has completely gone from his eyes. The front entry wooden planked floor has been freshly scrubbed and not only is there a void where the Michelangelo piece once was, the entire spot has been cleared of all its showy art-gallery displays. I avert my eyes from this area completely.

Sam leads me into the den where the three of us first sat and talked the other night. I never noticed a desk here before, but this is where Sam gestures me to sit. As I curl into the chair, keeping my arms and legs closely pinned to my torso, I observe the vast array of impressive medical school diplomas hanging on the walls. This is really more a home-office than a den, I think to myself.

Sam motions for me to take off my jacket and sunglasses, but I ignore him. He doesn't waste time.

"I didn't kill my wife."

The sentence just hangs there. I look at Sam to see if he's going to say more because I'm uncomfortable with silence but I'm not about to fill his intentional gap with my own uneasy prattle.

"Tell me the name of the website that Ruth told you she met her latest lover on."

"I think it was called *The Rare Affair*," I say and try not to squirm in my chair. Latest lover?

"Rare Affair, that's a new one," Sam says and I'm perplexed what he could mean by that. But he doesn't stop to explain.

"For the record, Ruth never told me she was leaving me. I know that is what you told the police and from that, they've concluded I flew into a crazed rage. But I'm here to tell you that it didn't happen," his voice is measured. "Furthermore, the police have located this fellow Scott, whom you claim to have seen at Boulder Creek, and have questioned him thoroughly. My lawyers say he's sticking to his story that Ruth just gave him a couple of quick blow jobs in his car—which if you think about it, makes sense so soon after childbirth." Sam stops to sigh deeply and I wonder why Ruth would describe her wild sexual escapades to me if there were none. But it was very much her nature to boast to me.

"This Scott dude is also married with no plans to leave his wife. So either she never intended to break that piece of news to me or there's someone else she's carrying on with. Perhaps someone who stopped her before she could talk. There are all sorts of loonies out there; maybe one of them became Ruth's lover," Sam concludes carefully. It's all I can do to muster a nod at his detailed and well thought out theory.

"Before I go explore Rare Affair, lemme just check her email," he says, typing rhythmically and clicking the mouse on his desk. "I've been monitoring her account ever since her . . . uh, just in case someone writes something significant to her."

I watch Sam look at Ruth's email and suddenly he grows very still and looks up to gaze at me contemplatively. I can't help it, out of nerves and now probably habit—a nervous habit—I reach for the lump on my left breast.

"What's the matter?" he asks, exceedingly alert to my small movement.

I make a quick decision. Better to sidetrack him with this, then have the conversation continue in the uneasy direction it's been headed.

"I have this lump," I say fretfully. Let him think all my tension today is due to cancer worries.

"Look, I asked you before to remove your sunglasses," he says gruffly. This time I comply.

Sam takes one last look at the computer screen then leans in close to me scrutinizing my face. I can smell his earthy, masculine scent.

"Well, well, didn't your black eye heal up fast!" Sam says with a facetious tone. Why does he bring that up now, I wonder.

Before I can give my standard make-up camouflage answer, Sam spins the computer monitor around and I find myself staring at a large photograph. It's me. Sitting by some flowers in our front yard at home. The photo was taken about a year ago because I'm wearing glasses and now I have tinted blue contact lenses which Nathan recently ordered for me. Contacts that are painful.

"Where did you get this?" I ask, confused.

"I just this moment downloaded it on Ruth's email," he answers. "It was sent this morning from your husband with a note saying, 'Have you seen this woman? She's missing and suffering from post-partum depression, possibly psychosis. She needs medication and any information is appreciated on her safe return'." Sam reads methodically, and then looks to me for my reaction.

"Well, certainly you don't think he would type, 'Please return my wife so I can blacken her other eye and maybe bust her jaw'," I retort. But now I'm worried. Psychosis? My god, how many people has Nathan sent that email to? And how many other people have they forwarded it on to? And so on, and so on, my own scary concept of infinity. And what must people think of me? Even though it seems like weeks, I've only been gone four days. Why can't Nathan just understand that I need a little time to process and accept things? I told him I was coming right back.

"You said you have a lump?" Sam sure stays focused.

I am now extremely uncomfortable with where this is heading, but there's nothing to do but nod yes.

"And you're telling me this because you know I'm a breast surgeon and you're afraid to go to another doctor and risk being recognized," he leads. I hadn't thought of any of that.

"Lay down," he says. "I can tell you in one minute."

What? I watch in disbelief as he gets up from the desk and ambles to the sofa. He's going to do a breast exam on me? I'm no longer capable of pre-screening my own thoughts and so I blurt out, "You're going to do a breast exam on me?"

"I can allay your fears," he says. "I'm certain of it."

I anxiously walk past him with my arms folded across my chest. Relax, Nordis, I tell myself. This time you'll be unbuttoning your own shirt. And you're not at a drive-in movie. And he's a highly respected doctor in his field. And he didn't laugh at your joke. And as a surgeon, he's seen lots of things before. And nobody cares that you're not back at your pre-pregnancy weight yet. I chastise myself—it's not always about you. (I hate when people say that.) This poor, sad man could go to prison for life and here he's trying to do you a favor.

But this is more than daunting for me. It's really, really scary. I lie down on the couch; a few shallow breaths catch in my throat as I slowly unbutton my blouse, feeling the silky material fall to each side.

Sam rubs his hands together in an effort to warm them (very considerate, really) and I open my front clasp bra and look up expectantly. What am I expecting?

He doesn't make physical contact, just kneels down and looks. Maybe he knows that I detest being touched. Or perhaps something he sees looks too revolting to handle. Can he diagnose me on sight alone?

"Someone did some very nice work here," he comments. "Beautiful." He looks me straight in the eyes. "But I'd say this is many years ago."

"Yes," I confirm, grateful to have something intelligent to say. "A reduction done in 1988." His eyes are soft and muted, gentle. His hands are large and masculine, but also gentle. Do I tell him I dreamed of his eyes and hands?

He reaches out and tells me to relax. He puts a flattened palm over my left breast and sweeps it across the surface of my skin. Then with the pads of just three fingers, he presses down, making firm, even, circular motions across the area I've indicated. I force myself not to recoil at his touch. He's touching me. Here. He's looking at me. Here.

This must be what women are made to submit to when they go to their gynecologists. I'm so repelled by my body, particularly my breasts, that I've avoided this procedure my entire life. But wait, he's saying something.

"This? This is nothing," he speaks in a reassuring tone but more to himself than to me. He then takes my left hand which has been resting at my side and squeezes it much too tightly between both of his.

"But Nordis, you are really something." That part he says louder.

"Excuse me?" I say.

That's when he leans down close, his face grazing my shoulder. At first I think he intends to lower his lips to my breasts, but he turns sharply toward my ear instead and whispers, "It's you."

Chapter 28

"Scene" But Not Heard

"I know it's you," Sam repeats again, probably because I don't respond.

Numbing, seismic shockwaves spread from the epicenter of my body to its outer edges. When people are this close in, I close down. Sam's proximity is smothering, suffocating and silencing.

"You killed her," his voice seethes through gritted teeth. "And then took off without another thought. What is wrong with you? I had a life. We had a life. Who the hell are you?" I feel woozy and all the food I gorged on feels hot and burning, rising up in my throat.

I can't believe I once tried to provoke Nathan into showing this type of passion by making him jealous. But now I'm frightened because Sam is a stranger. Nathan was safe, his responses fairly predictable. I cannot calculate Sam. How much does he know?

Sam jostles me but not so much in anger, as to urge me to respond. At least this is my initial assessment. Maybe I'm wrong and it's just the beginning of a violent rampage in which he explodes and inflicts everything on me that he's already been accused of doing to his wife. And wouldn't that be fitting? The urgent shaking of my shoulders transitions into excruciating pressure, which he applies to my forearms as he pushes them down into the couch. I feel the masculinity in his grip which is undeniably potent. Sam is draped over my body and bent over my face. Sam is everywhere. There is literally nowhere to focus my eyes that's not full of Sam. It's too bright in the room, so I scrunch my lids firmly together as I clutch at the couch, my fingernails scraping the nubby fabric in a pathetic attempt for pity. If he presses me down any harder, I'll go straight through the sofa. I can already feel the metal coils below, waiting to perforate my skin into ribbons. But Sam shows no sign of relenting. He presses, presses, compresses, compresses, depresses, suppresses, impresses, oppresses, represses, presses—and suddenly—without any warning . . . Stops! Sam completely releases his powerful grip on me and I can feel tingling as sensation returns to my arms.

For just a moment, lying there with my eyes closed, I think Sam might be gone. I don't feel him, see him or hear him anymore. But his strong musky, slightly spicy scent grows intoxicatingly closer and then . . . he breaks the silence with a low, guttural groan.

"I could kill you in a backwards minute. Minutes, hours, months, years. Time! Do you hear me? It's only time! I wouldn't have to do any more time than I'm already going to do. And I won't get my time back, will I? But I can take yours with me, can't I?" He goads me to answer but I'm too rigid with fear. "Can you spare the time? Miss, do you have the time?" Sam's unexpected and controlled politeness frightens me more than his prior wrath. I don't know what to do so I timidly look down at my watch and start to unbuckle the strap.

"I'm out of time!" Sam yells for the first instance this evening and I jump, my wristwatch falling to the floor. "That's right, a watch. My red watch," Sam bellows and smacks the sofa with his whole arm. "So easy, yet so clever. You plant my watch. And now I've killed my wife. Tick-tock."

He mashes his face next to mine and grimaces. "And smell this?" I inhale out of nerves and it makes me heady. "You should fucking love this scent. It's the aroma of your freedom."

I keep my head bowed, cowering at his booming voice. He has figured it all out now. Everything. My hiding the watch and spraying his cologne. Sam is right—I deserve his unleashed fury. But instead of more shouting, he roughly grabs my chin with his hand, tilting it up so our eyes are level. But mine are still closed.

"Look at me, goddamn it!" Sam roars. "Open your eyes."

At this moment, I vomit up all emotion. Every feeling, every fear, every sadness, every disappointment, every shame, every doubt, every embarrassment and every regret spurts out all over the sofa, staining it with my humiliation.

Convulsive sobs uncontrollably wrack my body and I'm sure my entire upper torso must look like jelly—or globs and blobs of heaving, glutinous cheesecake that can no longer be contained by the woven fabric of my blouse.

No words come out, just sound effects and motion. For I have a non-speaking part in this scene.

INTERIOR OF SAM'S OFFICE—AFTERNOON

NORDIS, bare-breasted and vulnerable, positioned awkwardly on the formal brocade sofa. The sunshine streams brazenly through the open curtains, highlighting every mark, blotch, mole, scab and scar on her immense body. On this particular day, the bright, unforgiving sun even seems capable of illuminating character flaws.

SAM, depleted and taken aback by the sudden scope of raw emotion that emanates from Nordis, drops his head down to rest on her chest. And this one tiny gesture seems to escalate Nordis' sobs. Sam waits several moments in this position until she hushes down to a slight whimper. He can hear her heartbeat. This is not a doctor moment, it is a human one.

SAM
(tenderly now)
I'm sorry. That was too much. That wasn't me.

Nordis swallows hard.

SAM
I think you should know there was one more photograph in that email. It's another one of you. With a baby.

Nordis freezes and forcefully shuts her eyes.

SAM
And underneath, your husband wrote, Urgent: Have you seen this woman and her infant son?

Nordis remains motionless, eyes closed, hoping this portion of the examination ends soon. Sam lifts his head up and looks at this troubled woman. A woman whose burdens are definitely not breast cancer related. He walks back to the desk and picks up a camera.

Nordis opens her eyes as he approaches with the camera. Flustered and suddenly remembering she's terribly exposed, she pulls together the silk from her blouse. She covers her face, recalling the blinding flash years ago from the Polaroid camera in Fuji's dress shop.

SAM
Shh, shh. Hey, you're okay, you're alright.
I'm not taking your picture.

Nordis thinks she can start to believe what Sam says. She directly meets his eyes for the first time since crying.

SAM
I just want to show you something that I
found in this camera. I didn't know what
to make of it last night. Now I do.

Nordis looks where Sam points, at the camera's mini viewfinder screen. Displayed in full color is a picture; a baby with a pinafore dress pulled up, and white ruffled pantaloons yanked down. The baby's diaper gapes wide open.

Sam zooms the shot in closer to magnify something. A small penis.

Nordis is quiet. She remembers the camera lying around the other day. The housekeeper had taken a picture of all four of them. When she went upstairs, Ruth must have snapped this photo as evidence.

SAM
Ruth knew, didn't she? And you knew that
Ruth knew. So you . . .

Nordis finds her voice for the first time.

NORDIS
Sam. It wasn't like that, Sam. Please believe me.
It was an accident. It's not like it seems.

SAM
Oh, nothing is what it seems. It seems to me
that you had a black eye from your abusive
husband. It seems to everyone else that you had
a daughter. It seems to your husband that you've
gone mad. And now it seems to the police that I've
killed my wife.

Nordis lets Sam vent what she hopes is the tail end of any remaining rage, then watches his expression soften again.

NORDIS
And it seems to me that you could just
possibly be the one person who understands.

Chapter 29

DEPTH PERCEPTION

I'm driving my car, but it's my mind that races full throttle. I don't know what to concentrate on first. Each individual thought revs its loud engine, gunning its motor to win over my attention. And when that black and white checkered flag raises, the accelerated noise in my head will be deafening.

Concentrate on the road, I command myself. I shouldn't be driving now. I'm not even insured on this rental car. When I'm upset, I lose my depth perception and can't tell how close I am in proximity to the vehicle in front of me. The same thing happens with people. I find it tricky to determine who I'm actually in a close relationship with or who simply appears to be close to me; but just like the sign on the side view mirror reads, "objects are closer than they appear," it's all just an illusion. Optical illusions. Do eye doctors like Nathan treat people for optical illusions? Do psychiatrists treat people for illusional thoughts? Maybe that's delusional thoughts. I'm all mixed up. I shouldn't be driving.

Sam does get me, I just know he does. The truth is that Sam understands, but only certain things. That's what he finally told me toward the end of the evening. Some things about this situation, about me, he can't begin to fathom and truthfully, neither can I. But it's nice to know that Sam and I both get the same things. We both understand that I am not psychotic and do not need to be on medication.

And Sam would be far more knowledgeable about this subject than Nathan because he almost became a psychiatrist. He told me tonight that he switched specialties in medical school to become a surgeon after his mother passed away from breast cancer. So he would know about things like that, almost being a shrink and all. Nathan fixes eyes. And when you're involved with eyes, you shouldn't go around emailing people about psyches and mental illness.

Perhaps you can divulge if someone is nearsighted or has an overly curved cornea, but that's about all you're really qualified to say.

Sam was very clear and concise with me tonight and by the end of it all, his face was weary. I understand that kind of fatigue. When there's a jigsaw puzzle and all the little pieces look identical and there's only one with that tiny, imperceptible difference that fits correctly into place. And you're so blurry eyed from repeated attempts that you finally take any jagged-shaped piece that remotely resembles the right silhouette; cut off a corner, flatten the side and create a whole new pointy tip. And then if you jam it in hard enough, it fits . . . sort of.

But there had been no way to wrap up what had happened these past two days into a tidy little package; no way to neatly complete the puzzle. And so after all my tears, our conversation naturally shifted into shared verbal intimacies. I guess that's what happens when you've already been physically vulnerable as I had—there's nothing left to do but finally trust. We talked for hours over wine, and I unveiled myself in many ways to Sam, disclosing details I never thought possible. Always, I waited for some sign of disapproval, some measure of criticism or some warning of repugnance. But none came.

It could've been the wine, but soon Sam reciprocated with a few of his own revelations. Ruth never told me she married Sam for family approval and security. Something she and I had in common, I think, remembering my first marriage. She also never told me this was her fourth affair. The three others were from a different website. She absolutely never mentioned that Sam was sterile and couldn't father any children and so she convinced him to let his brother be a donor so the child would still bear family resemblance. But Sam told me all these things and more tonight.

He even told me one night during the pregnancy, he was so unhappy in his marriage that he drank too much and called a telephone helpline one evening. Yes, yes he certainly did, I remember fondly.

I want to trust Sam but part of me thinks he had an ulterior motive by imparting his own personal information to me. Perhaps he's making himself seem more like a real and sympathetic person. So that I can't possibly maintain my story and leave him holding the bag. Even though the police have my airtight babysitting alibi and they have established a strong motive for him. And they have solid physical evidence with his watch and cologne too. But maybe Sam knows he will have something better. Maybe he knows he will have me. And he knows I have heart.

After the wine and the words, he had walked me slowly to the door. "Don't worry, plea bargaining will be your ticket. And the fact that you're a mother with no prior felonies," he told me.

Plea bargaining. Probably the first of many legal terms that will be in my vocabulary from now on. And I didn't waste any time doing it.

"Please, Sam. Give me a week before you call your lawyers," I pled as we stood by his front door. "You know I'm dealing with so much right now. I promise I'll make a formal confession, if you just give me some time to get things in order." I've always been good at bargaining.

"I'll call you tonight," he said and shut the door quietly. I stood there alone on that front porch, remembering the first time I arrived there, before I ever even met Sam, with my "black" eye and my little "girl." Just a mere three nights ago.

I'm now just blocks away from Brenna and the babies when I almost smash into a car. What is that, a Lexus? Sam drives a Lexus. But that's not Sam. He's probably home right now speaking to his high-powered attorney on the phone. Or the police. Or perhaps he's making funeral arrangements. That gives me pause. I really should confess prior to Ruth's funeral so Sam can attend. Nobody will let him near her memorial service if they think he killed her in cold blood. But I can't even begin to imagine what will happen to me. And my children. And will the sentencing be heavier when it's discovered I've lied? Do they take into consideration someone who panics? A panic plea?

I don't even have an attorney to call. I start to cry again but the tears just blur my vision, making things worse so I have to slam on my breaks because the car in front of me does an unexpected and illegal U-turn. I actually think all U-turns should be permissible. Who hasn't wanted to change their mind about the direction they're headed at some point in their life?

When I unlock my hotel room door, I'm shocked to discover the hushed blackness that envelopes me. I thought I'd find Brenna huddled next to the television, volume low or gabbing on her cell phone, like a typical teenager. I remind myself that she's not a typical teen. But I was at least certain I would walk in on one or both babies fussing and Brenna walking the floor, shoulders heavy with squalling infants. Instead, Brenna snuggles up to my baby (what?) while Bridget is swaddled tightly in a receiving blanket and propped against the headboard. And what is that sickly sweet smell? I look at the clock. No wonder they're exhausted, it's midnight. Did Sam and I really talk this long?

With the room dark and quiet, I decide to do something that I've been putting off. I decide to log onto the computer. With those sobering photos and that email Nathan sent to Sam today, (and god knows who else?) things seemed to have deteriorated greatly at home and I need to prepare myself for what's happening with Nathan. Perhaps I also need to prepare Nathan for what's about to happen to me.

Chapter 30

My World Wide Web

I haven't been on this computer since I first arrived in Colorado and wrote my lighthearted letter to Nathan explaining I had left for a little getaway. I've been avoiding email, just like the person who leaves her answering machine on to screen messages from undesirable callers. But now I know things are critical and Nathan could have the police in Los Angeles involved already. He might even tell them he thinks I'm suicidal or that I could hurt our baby, and they'd believe him. There's no telling what he might do, especially if my mother girlishly whispers tall tales from my past into his receptive ear. I need to find out what I'm up against with him.

I glance once more at the drowsy occupants in this room. How nice if I could have the innocence of a baby or the clear conscience of a sixteen year old and be able to sleep soundly tonight, not fretful over what will happen to me in a jail cell. Locked up.

I sit at the little desk and almost choke on my emails when I see just how many have filled my inbox. I don't even know where to start. But then I see one from Jane.

Dear Wondrous Nordis,

Do not imprison yourself. Be free.

Love,
Jane

ps. You don't smell like tuna anymore.

I knew it! I knew there was something about her. This was Jane, my best friend from fourth grade who refused to sit next to me in the school cafeteria. Tears spring to my eyes, more from current anxiety than old childhood hurts. I reread her email and a slight comforting warmth pervades my body, but I tell myself not to get too hopeful yet. Jane doesn't know anything—she just has uncanny . . . uncanny what? Timing, I think. I want to contemplate this more, but I must read the other emails. I decide to start with the most predictable—my mother.

> *Nordis,* (**I notice there's no "dear" here)**
>
> *How could you be so selfish as to up and leave your husband (a man who works hard day and night to keep you in the style to which you have become accustomed) and your twins (boys who were already feeling twinges of jealousy over a new sibling) in such a terrible lurch like this? Not to mention my eldest grandson who, because he's such a sensitive young man, suffers terribly all alone right now. If this is another one of your "tests" to find out who cares about you (like when you hid inside the clothes dryer for eight hours when your brother was born) you've gone way too far. Remember this . . . "Our character is what we display when we think no one is looking." There is only so much nonsense a fine man like Nathan can be expected to tolerate before he walks. Perhaps with another woman, even. I would think that in your thirty-six years, you would've developed some maturity and consideration for how your actions impact others. "For every action, there is an equal and opposite reaction."* (**She's quoting scientists now.**) *If I had ever married a husband even half as decent as Nathan, I would stay by his side, morning, noon and . . .*

At that point I hit the delete button. I can take her lectures but I can't stand her putting down my poor father who isn't even around to defend himself anymore. If only it were this easy to delete her other behaviors. But immediately I wish I hadn't trashed her letter. Something about her tone toward Nathan makes me uneasy. She's always fawned over him but now there appears to be something else written between the lines. I can't put my finger on it just yet.

Next I click on a letter from Nathan that, like the email from my mother, is also dated the first day I left. It screams, "URGENT" in the subject heading.

Hello Nordis,

Please call me ASAP—Justin has a high fever and might need to go to the hospital. Your tireless mother continues to help us. Please come home.

Nathan

Justin! I sit and stare at this email and it frightens me. And makes me feel horribly guilty. I snatch up the hotel phone but then I consider something. Brenna has just been to my home and if Justin were sick, she would've told me. I'm more and more certain this is a nasty ploy designed to bring me home because Nathan knows how much I worry. Cruel, manipulative behavior, that's what this is.

And then there's this offhand reference to my mother in his email. My mind wanders as I look at Brenna's hair splayed out on the pillow. My mother and Nathan both mention one another in their emails. My mother tried to convince Brenna to let her adopt Bridget? But why? I slam my eyes shut to think. I reflect back to my pregnancy; those exhausting nights when my head hung low before I could even clear the table, let alone make love to my husband. Many nights I would go to bed early, leaving them to play games or just play . . . My mother always around, always helpful, always fussing over Nathan when I couldn't. Could my mother be planning to be with Nathan? Could she somehow be thinking that if she had a baby, she'd stand a better chance with him? I can see it in my mind's eye, her mini-skirt parade (because she still has nice legs) her gin rummy skills (Nathan loves that game) and her baked yams. (Nathan's favorite.) Yes, all she's missing is the baby and she'd have her man.

Or is Nathan in on this too? Was that Nathan's voice on the other end of the phone when my mother received that call while she was at Brenna's home? Could the two of them be plotting to run off with one another and start a family of their own? My mother is an attractive woman and she has always said motherhood was the best time of her life. I can't even think about this, their possible entanglement. It's all so ugly.

I really need someone to talk to about this. I consider waking Brenna. Instead I open up the next email. I'm surprised to see the name of one of my old therapists as the sender.

Dear Nordis,

Your husband recently called to alert me to the current turmoil in your life. I've reviewed your file and it appears that we haven't had a visit in quite some time, a year ago to be exact when I helped you come to terms with your father. I do think it would be wise, under the circumstances, for us to have a telephone session as soon as possible.

Please call me at your earliest convenience.

Susan Popham

Well, Nathan was right to pick Susan out of all five shrinks I've seen in recent years. But what can she say to help me now? I think of Susan, eyeglasses in hand as she'd rub her tired brows and say, "Nordis, let's think about that in greater depth. I think your perception of that incident might be slightly distorted." I rather liked Susan because she never tried to talk me into antidepressants and she always celebrated my creativity and my unique way of looking at life. I'm feeling slightly ashamed for some of the times I embellished a story, or made up an exciting incident because I thought she seemed bored in our sessions. Maybe I could call Susan now. What am I thinking? My next phone call needs to be to a lawyer.

My mind reverts back to Sam and our evening. Should I send him a quick email thanking him for giving me the consideration of more time? But if he hasn't decided to do that, he'll only see that as calculating on my part. On the other hand, why would he care if just a few more days go by before I'm arrested? Arrested. I shudder at the thought of metal handcuffs. I forge ahead and open the next email for distraction.

Dear Mrs. Spect,

This is your weekly report reflecting your son Michael's progress here at Evergreen Canyon Rehab. Michael has only had one incident this month and that was when he punched his roommate in the stomach for withholding some mail that came for him. Last month's arson episode has been discussed thoroughly, in both a group setting and with his therapist, and Michael appears to take responsibility for his actions. His grades have remained at the C level. Michael continues to be more open with his feelings that stem from your divorce, and also his emotions surrounding his grandfather. It is the hope of all concerned that he will persist in taking further steps to explore these issues. Visitation this month will commence on the first and third weekends. Your next official update will be sent in one week.

Sincerely,
The caring Staff at Evergreen Canyon Rehab

I quickly close this email. I have been putting this issue on the backburner until I can obtain some clarity with it. My ex-husband and I have disagreed from the start how to handle our son's downward spiral. He had been doing so wonderfully ever since our move to Los Angeles and I know he embraced my marriage to Nathan. You couldn't ask for a better stepfather. But ever since my Dad, his grandfather . . . well that seemed to retrigger the trauma. I just miss him terribly, that's all. Where did the little boy who used to sit on my lap and read *"Poky Little Puppy"* go? It's like a fatality for me. The death of his innocent, childlike, affectionate nature.

I look over at this new slumbering baby, so sweet and innocent. Why couldn't you just have been born a gentle little girl, I silently implore the baby who snuggles under Brenna's chest. But I can't go down this path right now. I must stay focused on the present.

The last email I open for the night (though there are about forty more) is from my life-long friend Gail and I realize that I haven't spoken to her since the evening she and the others came over to see my baby. I remember overhearing her as I pretended to be sound asleep on the sofa. She had expressed concern that I hadn't named my baby yet. Yes, Gail is a good and caring friend. Someone I can trust.

Dear Nordie,

I called your house tonight after receiving that distressing email flier with those photos saying that you have run off with the baby. How awful! I talked to Nathan and he confirmed everything. I thought we were close friends, Nordie. How come you didn't call me with any of this? I would've been there for you. I have to say I was rather hurt when Nathan told me that he's sending your newest friend Brenna (**He sent Brenna?!**) *to track you down and work on bringing you home. He says she's the only one you trust nowadays. That's very upsetting to me after the road we've been down together, Nordis. I've seen you through a divorce and your father, so I can't believe you wouldn't turn to me at a time like this. How did you meet this girl? Nathan said you became acquainted at a hospital. An eye patient of his?* (**Nathan's patient?!**) *I think you should return home and take those pills that Nathan told me your mother says you need. Call me when you get back and we'll meet for coffee. The girls want to plan a mom's night out to go see that girly flick, I think it's called . . .*

I stop reading because I'm dazed. Nathan's patient? What? Brenna never told me that she had eye surgery in Nathan's office. Brenna and Nathan knew one another? I look at Brenna and her long eyelashes seem to flutter in her sleep. Did those pretty eyes once have problems? Could she have betrayed me? Nathan and Brenna? Oh my god. My heart races. Did Nathan meet Brenna in his practice, find himself attracted to her and then sleep with her, resulting in a pregnancy? I think back to the state of my marriage then. It was rocky, yes. That must be why he offered her money for the doctor. He cares because he knows this is his baby. And now my mother is working on his behalf, trying to get his baby so they can go off and raise it together. This definitely seems possible based on what I know of my mother and also because she so often declares her devotion to her "fine son-in-law." She would help him if he requested it. Certainly.

My mind shifts into cruise control as it whirls around the racetrack for the second time tonight. I turn this theory over and over in my head, having it make more sense each time around. That must be it. But that can't be it. Brenna has always maintained she doesn't know who the father is. I always assumed perhaps she was a bit promiscuous in her junior year at high school and . . . wait a second. Maybe Brenna doesn't know who fathered her baby, but Nathan does know. And the reason he knows is because he raped her. You read about this all the time. A surgeon will have his way with a female patient while they're under anesthesia, right there in the operating room. They never even remember it happening. Maybe just their clothing is arranged slightly different, but other than that, how would they know? I think of Nathan's faithful nurse, Polly. Would she look the other way for a thing like this to happen? My god, what am I thinking? I'm losing my perspective after everything I've been through. My mind is now in overdrive. I reread the first part of Gail's email.

What is this about Nathan sending Brenna to find me? It was Brenna's and my own idea for her and Bridget to come here. Wasn't it? Or did she just let me think that? Is she reporting back to Nathan? Could Brenna be as skilled at lying as . . . I stop when I realize the rest of the sentence is "I am." I think I may be getting slightly paranoid in my thinking. Or as my therapist used to say, my perception of this situation has become a bit distorted. "Check out the reality," she always told me. "Don't just presume." With this in mind, I check the computer's outbound folder. I would like nothing better than to be proven wrong.

Sure enough, there is an email sent to Nathan with today's date. I know it wasn't me who wrote to Nathan tonight. I don't think I want to see this but I click my mouse and the words burst onto the screen.

Dear Dr. Spect,

It's too late to call but I think there's something else you should know. After we talked, your wife left me to baby-sit. I had to look around the hotel room for a new nipple because the one left for me cracked and the baby was hungry. In a corner behind the desk were bags of baby girl's clothes and hair ornaments, even shoes. I also found some professionally taken photographs of Nordis holding your son but he was wearing girl's clothing. I am very concerned about your wife but have not had a chance to talk with her yet.

Please call me on my cell phone.

Sincerely yours,
Brenna

I look up at this young girl, now smiling in her sleep, and I can only think one thing. I never told Brenna my joke. It's time she hears it.

Chapter 31

WHEN SKIES ARE GRAY

I race to the punchline. ". . . have a little mustard, the doctor says!" I pause.

Brenna doesn't laugh. But this doesn't necessarily make her sincere, it just makes her sleepy. She stares at me, rubbing crust from her lashes. Finally she confesses.

"Nordis, I did something while the babies were sleeping. I wrote to Nathan tonight. I'm really worried about stuff. And you."

"Why didn't you tell me Nathan sent you here in the first place, Brenna?"

"What difference does it make how I got here? The point is I am here and you need a friend."

"Brenna. Brenna!" I say, feeling my voice rise. "It makes all the friggin difference in the world. You don't get what's happening." I notice that I talk younger when I'm around her.

She starts to cry softly. At first I think it's one of the babies, but then I see it's her. Poor kid. I can calm myself down and so I do.

"Look, I'll drop this," I say with forced kindness. "Just tell me one thing. Does Nathan know the name of this hotel?"

Brenna looks to the side and nods undetectably. I perceive her reluctance to answer as positive affirmation and seize the nearest suitcase.

"I called him tonight after you left and read him the address from the hotel stationary," she admits overtly now. At least she's honest and doesn't cover up her tracks. Like me.

"We're outa here," I say, remaining composed so as not to frighten her or wake the babies prematurely. "Help me pack." I toss random nearby items into the duffel bag; make-up, clothing, baby bottles, diapers, formula, blankets, books, and cupcake boxes all zoom inside.

"What are you afraid of?" Brenna asks. There's no time to tell her of tonight's adoption theories or other complicated ideas, so I promise I'll catch her up in the car. But Brenna catches me first. Completely off guard.

"Nordis, Bridget was really sick tonight. I put her on that end of the bed in case she was contagious. She wouldn't stop throwing up." That's the odor in here, I think. Brenna seems concerned but not the extreme apprehension a more experienced mother would display, knowing a vomiting infant could lead to quick and severe dehydration. And isolating a baby is not the thing to do either.

I rush over to the bed where I see the poor little thing slumped down, supported only by the taut wrapping of the baby blanket. I remember the nurse showing us how to swaddle them like that in the hospital and Brenna did a good job. For me it was a refresher course, but this was all new territory for a sixteen year old. As is most everything for her, I'm slowly realizing. I can't be angry with Brenna. This is all Nathan, he's the adult.

Little Bridget is pasty and her breathing and pulse seem slow to me. We've got to get her to a doctor, I think, without panicking Brenna. But the first order of business is to check out of here before Nathan can come and detain me with his false kidnapping accusations. Or worse—before he can convince some official that I'm crazy and have my baby removed completely. That's just what he'd like to do. Have the baby for himself so he can raise it with my mother's nurturing and overly capable influence.

I realize that checking-out by phone is the most expedient way and after I hang up with the front desk, we wake both babies to bundle them up. I can see through the darkened window that it's snowing outside.

The babies, upset at being jarred from their warm cocoons, holler in a high-pitched frantic way that makes us scurry urgently around, jostling one another in our tight quarters. But we don't have time to feed them, or do we? I ask Brenna to approximate when she talked to Nathan on the phone and then I calculate flight times. Yes, we can feed these babies.

My baby greedily sucks down his bottle but Bridget jerks spastically, retching and shunning away from Brenna's breast until both mother and baby collapse into the bedcovers, a heap of sobs. I trade babies and try to console the screaming, scrawny, itty-bitty thing with my finger in her mouth. To my amazement she quiets down and her large dark pupils seem to dilate in the dim light as she gazes straight at me with what seems like wonderment in her eyes. I brush my lips over the fuzzy wisps on her head and breathe in that very familiar baby scent. I'm holding a little girl, I think.

For some reason Brenna asks what my baby's middle name is and I'm caught off guard. How do I tell her there's not even a first name yet? Instead I deflect the question and ask what Bridget's middle name is.

"Ray. Bridget Ray. Because she's a little ray of sunshine."

I begin singing everyone a lullaby but mostly it's to lull myself. "You are my sunshine, my only sunshine, you make me happy, when skies are gray . . ." I never liked songs about the sun, but I guess her middle name triggers it. Brenna is delighted with this melody and joins in.

I switch to humming and let Brenna carry the tune. I'm realizing that I never heard from Sam tonight and he was supposed to call and let me know if he would give me a little time before he turned his evidence in. Please, Sam.

I think about calling my old therapist now and just giving it to her straight. But what would I say? "Sue, this is Nordis and I'm in an awful mess. You probably don't know this, but back when I came to you for depression, sometimes I used to make up a few events just to interject a little liveliness into our sessions because I thought I was a boring client. They were harmless tales and it was probably just the creative part in me. Tonight, it's not so harmless, and what I've created is heartbreak."

But I don't do this. Instead, I load my arms with all our belongings and use the stroller Brenna brought for the overflow. We take the elevator and look at one another as the doors slide shut. Elevators are always awkward with another person, even if you're inside with a friend. It's the sudden and silent closure as if you might be entombed with them forever that make it odd. I force conversation.

"Bridget will be alright," I say calmly. "We'll take her to the emergency room." But then I wonder how to do that without someone recognizing me. Either from the emails Nathan seems to have blanketed the country with or the information Sam may have already supplied the local authorities with. I just have to hope for the best because there's no turning back now. The baby's health is the most important priority.

The elevator doors hum open and we run smack into a maid that I recognize has been extraordinarily nice to me and the baby during our stay; leaving extra blankets and dropping off room service treats. She blocks the elevator with an outpouring of compliments for the tiny bundled babies, seemingly oblivious that one of them is very ill. Brenna clumsily rearranges some packages and something clanks to the floor. Thin, beige liquid oozes out of a sack onto the lobby marble floor.

"Oh, Nordis, I'm sorry. It's Charlie's formula. I hope you have more for him?" inquires Brenna.

"Him? Charlie!" The maid jerks to attention. "I thought this little darling was Ava Rose?"

Brenna looks away embarrassed as the maid moves inquisitively closer to us. I try to think fast but nothing comes to mind except to tell her the other baby is really sick and ask where the nearest hospital is.

Suddenly I feel a rough arm on my shoulder and turn to look up into Sam's serious eyes.

"I called a half hour ago and they told me you'd checked out?" His grip tightens on my shoulder. "Running off?"

Chapter 32

THE DOCTOR IS IN

Of course Sam concludes that I'm fleeing town, maybe even the country in an effort to elude arrest. And now I know enough about Sam not to try and convince him that this isn't what it seems. "Nothing is as it appears to be," would only sound like one of my mother's foolish quotations.

Instead, I shoo the maid away and beckon Brenna over. I pull back the pink blankie from Bridget's teeny face so Sam can peer in at her.

"This is one very sick baby," he says with authoritative alarm.

"Sam, this is the friend I told you about, Brenna. We don't know what's wrong with her daughter," I say, looking up at Sam's vexed expression.

Sam thoroughly inspects Bridget for several minutes. He looks carefully at the back of her neck, and in particular her ears, finger and toenails.

"Brenna, Sam is a physician, a surgeon actually," I say as explanation for his lengthy scrutiny.

"Ladies, may I offer an escort to the hospital?" Sam asks. The expression that passes over Brenna's face tells me she's now thoroughly frightened.

Sam drives my rental car since that is where the two carseats are and I remember the carseat defense he initially came up with which caused the detectives to interrogate me so profusely. I suppose if it wasn't logistics, something else would've given me away eventually.

In the hotel parking lot, I gasp when I catch a glimpse of Nathan and my mother circling around looking for a free space in an unfamiliar car. Using hand gestures and eye expressions, I noiselessly communicate to Brenna, and unbeknownst to Sam, both of us slither low in our seats until our car darts safely into the street. I silently pray that if Nathan makes inquiries as to my whereabouts, nobody in that hotel will mention a hospital. Aren't there privacy laws in this state?

There's no conversation as we drive but I notice Sam speeds and when a siren sounds in the distance, I panic. What happens if we get pulled over and Sam decides to point the finger at me right now. Tonight? I'm so fearful of what is going to happen to me that my stomach starts to churn and I realize I'm steadily twitching my left leg back and forth as it crosses over my right. I do that when I'm really disturbed.

The sirens seem to be about four young men alongside the curb. Just teenage boys really, who probably aren't authentic gang members but know how to give a pretty good imitation as two policemen pat them down. I look at their grungy clothes, unkempt hair, and disrespectful mouths spewing belligerence, and sigh at what seems an inevitable future when you have four boys. I look down at my little guy, sleeping so innocently in his padded bucket seat. I can't even fathom that one day he'll be shaving and drinking beer, let alone, stealing, swearing, watching pornography, and beating people up.

We're lucky that Sam takes us to the hospital in Boulder where he has residency and he's able to bypass the waiting room and get us seen immediately. Sam seems to know the on-call emergency room physician and I overhear lots of technical terms being tossed around. I recognize that this isn't a cold, flu or normal babyhood illness. There is talk of MRI's, CT scans and Gastrointestinal x-rays. I turn my head so Brenna does not see the tears I shed. I'm crying for such a tiny baby to have to endure so many big tests. I don't think Brenna is aware of what is about to take place. They show her where she can spend the night right next to Bridget and she looks very relieved not to be separated from her. They insert an intravenous line and we are all asked to give blood for a possible transfusion which we do.

Things seem grave.

After I give Brenna a huge hug, I lean over and give baby Bridget a gentle kiss. I walk down the long corridor with Sam. He's straight with me.

"That baby girl shows classic signs of Trisomy."

I've heard this word before but can't think what it is right away. Sam explains that Trisomy is a genetic chromosomal abnormality. Down's syndrome is the most common form it manifests, he elaborates, as we round a corner but that isn't what they suspect tonight. I'm so relieved to hear this because I know how serious Down's is for a child. But then he tells me Trisomy 18 or 13 are what Bridget presents with and further tests will be needed to diagnose. He adds that babies with this defect are not considered compatible with life and rarely survive for more than a few weeks. Not compatible with life? I must look devastated because Sam tells me nothing is for sure and to keep the faith. He then gives my hand a tight squeeze while I tighten the grip on my own sleeping baby.

Where are we going? As Sam drives, I'm wondering how much I should be talking. I'm afraid to say too much like I think I did with him before. I'm also afraid of saying too little. I decide to tell Sam that my husband was looking for me at the hotel earlier and for personal reasons, I really cannot go back there.

"Is that why you were checking out?" he asks.

I nod and so does he.

"I wasn't leaving town," I offer.

He takes his eyes off the road to look at me.

"Earlier you asked me for more time to get your personal affairs in order," Sam says.

"Yes. Please. I'm so scared."

"I've been thinking everything over. Everything we talked about earlier this afternoon," he announces. This is a good sign.

"I've decided to give you three days." Sam reaches toward me with his palm face up. "If you give me one night."

Chapter 33

OPTICAL "ALLUSIONS"

I can stall better than anyone I know. I linger in the darkened Manning nursery and think my typical "what if" thoughts. What if while both Nathan and my mother are here in Boulder, Nathan left the twins with his own inept mother? What if she watches her television shows and lets them run amuck and they get hurt like last time? Quickly, I pick up the extension that's on the wall and dial my phone number. It feels unfamiliar to push those digits and I realize how long it's been since I've called home.

"Good evening, Spect residence?" It's my mother-in-law's voice; she always answers phones with a questioning lilt. I can hear the Jeopardy theme song droning in the background. I'm about to hang up when I hear small voices.

"Grandma, Jarrett hit me!"

"Did not. Justin spit on my shoes."

"Hello is anyone on the line?" my mother-in-law persists, "Stop it the both of you or I'm calling your father. Hello? I can't hear anyone!"

I linger for another moment then disconnect the line. This is really the first time I've thought of the twins to any extent since I've left and the pangs of guilt start to hit. Why don't I miss them more? Maybe because it has been such a whirlwind here. But what if they don't even miss me? Worse, what if they haven't even noticed I've been gone? They're such Daddy's boys. They want Nathan to do everything with them and for them. I suppose I'm rather jealous because it seems Nathan is the one with the strong ties to the children and I attribute that to their all being male.

In fact, even my eldest son before we sent him away, preferred Nathan's company to mine. Nathan's cell phone was even the one called when Michael was expelled from school for the fire. Nathan picked him up and the two of them went somewhere to talk, where it was ultimately decided to keep the expulsion hush-hush from me, his own mother, for weeks. I can feel the resurgence of anger just thinking about this. Really, if you can't trust your husband and first-born, who is left? What if Nathan cultivates new secrets with the twins and eventually with this baby too? What if I'm always on the outside of my own family circle? What if this new baby had been a girl? I would have someone too.

Then like raging home intruders, the more serious "what-ifs" break into my hypothetical brain. What if Bridget dies? What if nobody believes me that Ruth's death was an accident? No, no, stop right there—I vigorously force those thoughts out the back door.

I feel surreal standing in Ruth's house without her, but even more so tucking my baby into her child's crib. Apparently since Ruth's death, Caden has been staying with Sam's brother because the sister-in-law is a stay-at-home mom and better able to care for him while Sam deals with his case. To my utter surprise, earlier tonight Sam mentioned relinquishing custody permanently to both of them now that Ruth is gone—his brother being the paternal father and all. Crash! Another thought assault . . . What if it's me who is put away for life—who will care for my own children? Of course the answer is quite obvious but I can't bear to think of all the platitudes she'll teach them. "Unless there is order in yourself, there can be no order in the world," she'll lecture while plying them with graham crackers.

As I carefully close the door to my sleeping baby, I can hear Sam's muffled voice in the distance talking on the phone. It seems to come from his office/den. My first inclination is to creep up close and eavesdrop. Surely I'd be able to find out exactly what he really thinks of me by listening. What if he's telling the police he has me in his custody and they should come over right now for the arrest? What if he's telling a colleague from the mental health field what a sick, crazy, sorry individual I am? Or what if he's telling a confidante on the other end that he desires me greatly?

I realize that I'm equally uncomfortable with all of these options and instead I wander into the upstairs bathroom and glimpse my reflection in the mirror. I hate mirrors but I haven't taken a close look at myself since I manufactured that bruised eye with my makeup. Hideous. I look like a swollen monster with three dimensional puffed-out, under eye circles and sagging jowls. Do I really look like this? No amount of fasting will negate this. Sometimes I inadvertently glimpse my reflection in a store mirror and I'll briefly admire my appearance, thinking I look pretty good for a woman my age. But not tonight. Tonight I'm able to trace the evidence of every sugary carbohydrate I've ingested these past few days in Colorado. Am I the only woman who has actually gained weight after giving birth? Enough mirror brutality. With a parting rueful look, I slip into the long hallway. What is this room?

This must be Ruth's craft retreat. I can see she's worked on painting, quilting and glassblowing here. Her efforts are exquisite. I realize some of the art downstairs that I took for famed originals were actually Ruth's own creations. She also has a corner of the room set up for her writing. I've forgotten that Ruth was an author and has published in many magazines. There was always friendly classmate rivalry between us in high school—who could write the better poem or short story? I meander to her desk and am surprised to see lots of her printed articles culled from folders. It looks as if someone has pored through these papers recently. Perhaps Sam has been rereading her deepest thoughts in an effort to keep her near to his heart. Or maybe there are things he never read before and he wants to find out who his wife really was. That's the thing about personal writing, it can outlast and outcast you.

I snoop at the paper on top and realize this is Ruth's account about having an affair. I feel a little guilty but it isn't like I'm reading her diary or anything. Is it?

Chapter 34

Ruth's Story

It's interesting to me that Ruth's story is written from a narrator's point of view. This is something I do when I want to distance myself from an event. I wonder if Ruth does the same? I look over my shoulder to make sure nobody is around, then pick up the first page and furtively begin to read . . .

One day Ruth thought about having an affair. This baffled her because she hadn't even been married that long. In fact, it was hard to differentiate if she was even married or she was just involved in a roommate relationship. There was her marriage certificate safely tucked in her nightstand drawer and the expensive wedding video with the embarrassing garter scene, covered with dust and sitting next to the crystal clock on the mantle. Definite proof of holy matrimony. But there was also a posted schedule of whose turn it was to take out the garbage and shop for the milk. Clear evidence of a roommate situation.

Truth be told, since she had her last milestone birthday, she'd thought about, toyed with, and contemplated the idea of an affair. But even though she'd reached this pivotal age, a potential affair wasn't because she was having a mid-life crisis. She certainly didn't long for a bright red sports car or to go skydiving. This had nothing to do with low self-esteem, she reassured herself. She looked pretty damn good for her age. No, these feelings were quite the opposite. She knew she deserved more than she was getting. She needed someone who understood her, who connected, who responded to her on a very profound and intuitive level. Without this in her life, she just felt dead inside. She could swear that she married someone who initially provided all this, but now she wonders if she was misled. The jury is still out as to whether she was intentionally duped by her altruistic, yet smooth talking husband (after all, he was a decade and a half older than her) or there just wasn't a long enough engagement period. She remembered how it felt to introduce him as her fiancé, the doctor. But one thing is certain—things now are vastly different than they were back then and impressing people just isn't as important to her anymore.

    She has tested the waters lately and made more intense eye-contact with attractive strangers. When they've returned her steady gaze, she's felt that elusive thrill from her college days. She remembers how she could easily turn a man's head back then with her long blonde hair. But her actions have never gone beyond this type of innocent flirting. Until today. She passed an interesting billboard with the name of a website on it. It advertised that married people who are "looking" can make contact with others with a similar mindset. "And then what?" she wondered. Visions of hang-up phone calls, excuses to get milk (when it wasn't even her turn) and seedy motel rooms ran through her head.

    When she first visited the website, she was captivated by the many photographs openly displayed. These men did not look underhanded, sleazy or desperate. They looked like men in her husband's social circle of professionals. They talked of voids. Mistakes, regrets and soul-searching were other buzzwords. Everyone stated in their profiles that they didn't want to change their current marital situation; they didn't want to hurt their lifelong partner or upset the family applecart. They promised complete discretion. They just wanted to supplement their life. "Monogamy is monotony" was their slogan.

    She found herself extremely attracted to several of the profiles but there was no way to contact them (even to innocently chat) without making a profile of her own. She could easily do this, especially with all her writing experience. And she had that one email account that her spouse never checked. Amazingly enough, even though she was always the one taking the pictures, she had a nice photograph of just her alone. She wouldn't even have to crop out someone else's arm around her. She decided in a split second to just do it. It was only a couple hundred words describing her likes and dislikes. What was the harm? She was careful to phrase things so people knew she hadn't done this before. She was not a player. She was just curious about what, or more to the point, who was out there. When she was done, she previewed it and felt secure that she would be getting a lot of views and correspondence. She hesitated for just a moment but then she clicked "Post" very matter of factly. After all, she wanted to have an affair. Didn't she?

Later on, she was glad she went ahead with publishing her profile because her husband was completely self-absorbed that evening. He didn't listen to anything she had to say and instead simply thought up the next clever remark he could interject or the next surgery he could boast over. She was tired of being talked over and around so that night when it was time to retire, she was grateful there wasn't any talking at all. She was careful to stay on her own side of the bed so as not to accidentally touch her husband. She wasn't in the mood for make-up sex.

What she really wanted to do was check her email. Carefully she slipped out of bed like a prisoner who escaped her bars and padded barefoot to the computer. It glowed eerily in the darkened den where just a few hours ago, she read a magazine while her husband researched a patient's case. She was rewarded and flattered when she found six new emails. Several of them tried to be funny. They tried too hard. One went on and on about himself, obviously self-absorbed. One talked about the extreme guilt over doing this, which she hadn't wanted to be reminded of. Two of them oozed and gushed over her photos and told her they wanted to sleep with her yesterday. This was the kind of desire she needed to feel. The pure, raw animalistic urge that was impossible to restrain. Her husband was far too gentle, far too tender and truthfully it felt like she was in bed with an overgrown boy scout.

She wrote back confidently to all six respondents. She asked bold questions. What brought them here? What exactly were they looking for? What was wrong with their marriage? She didn't ask anything she wasn't willing to answer herself. She told each one of them to write back and tell her something surprising, even shocking about themselves. She spent the next twenty minutes diligently deleting emails, emptying recycle bins, erasing history and otherwise covering her tracks as her husband slept peacefully in the next room. This was kind of daring, kind of thrilling and definitely an adventure into the unknown.

The next morning she couldn't and wouldn't look her husband in the eye, but interestingly, there was no real notice taken of this as he pored over lab results for his surgery that day. Everything proceeded as usual and she was off to her office where she was employed as a legal secretary. In the lobby of the building where she worked, she looked around and wondered how many people themselves had secret and elicit affairs. From the sheer population and number of hits on that website, she guessed it was one out of every three people. Was that one doing it? Maybe him? Oh! She would bet it was those two over by the ATM machine. Actually, that one over there could've possibly been one of her actual respondents—after all, the photo sent was faraway and *rather fuzzy. She felt giddy with anticipation and her day flew by. She never dared check her email from work because she'd heard employers could track things like that. Untraditional things.*

She raced home to log on. Jackpot! Ten new responses and four from the first batch had already written back. And with cell phone numbers. She thought about taking this to the next level . . . the world of sound, of voice, and laughter, but as a writer she felt more comfortable keeping it on the computer screen. As per her request for surprising tidbits, there were some real shockers and true confessions revealed. Someone was a divorce lawyer who seduced his clients. Someone else was happily married and was looking to add a threesome to their routine, while another someone had a gambling problem and lost their house. She noticed how that one original e-mailer who was so cocky and self-assured the first time had not sent a photograph yet or said anything astonishing. All the rest were interesting enough and it was odd to see how quickly things got personal when there was anonymity. But it was those voids in that one particular email that intrigued her the most. She ignored the other blatant attempts at intimacy from the rest and pursued the individual who was obviously holding something back. She loved a challenge.

Two weeks had passed and she was still wild with desire for this elusive stranger. She was very close to meeting him in the flesh, she felt it. There was such humor and his clever and witty remarks were like nothing she'd experienced, well at least not since she first got married. This man gave her his undivided attention. And he alluded to having a very respectable and important career so obviously he was a busy man as well. It thrilled her to no end that their online relationship took precedence. But after all this time, she still hadn't seen a photograph of him. She hardly minded because the mystery of it all was exactly what her tedious little life needed.

The more obsessed she became, the more she couldn't believe her spouse didn't notice. Did she want him to notice? Her computer time had increased three-fold and she barely slept. She was jumpy, edgy and euphoric all at the same time. She shopped for the perfect meeting outfit. There was talk of getting together for cocktails with the mystery man at an out-of-the-way place but she knew that would just be a pretense, a formality until they would simultaneously seduce one another physically, mirroring what had already transpired online.

Today's email had been especially clever and funny. A promise had been made that when they met, he would finally give her his photograph. She chuckled at how ironic that would be. And then, the email continued, he would tell what quality about her was the most attractive. She wrote back that she couldn't wait for this to happen then quickly deleted that because it made her sound desperate. Instead, with what she hoped sounded like just the right amount of casualness, she typed "perhaps our paths will cross one day when we're least expecting it." And she finished the email by telling him she looked forward to his photograph and the compliment when that time came.

She logged off the computer, sighed and sat quietly for a few moments thinking. When she walked out of the office and into the next room, she was startled to bump into her husband. As she looked up into his wistful eyes, a photograph was gently placed in her hand and he softly whispered, "It was your honesty that was the most attractive, Ruth."

Chapter 35

THE SAM EXAM

As I turn over the last page, I am stunned by the ending. Could this be a true story? I think back—did Ruth ever write fiction? But if anyone knows about the blurring of the lines between reality and imagination in writing, it's me. Only Sam knows if this is true. I'm also incredulous at the type of feelings she has expressed and how many of them echo my own sentiments. Had we been more alike than I realized? Perhaps that's why we were always so competitive back in school.

As I reread passages, I begin to wonder if this isn't a common experience shared by most married people at some point in their lives. Perhaps it's even universal? But if that's the case, wouldn't we all be having affairs? This must be where integrity, honor and respect come in. I remember the Fuji dress shop owner saying Nordis Spect = No Respect. I recall my ex-husband's sexual tryst with his company psychiatrist and how I felt at that betrayal. I remember trying to make Nathan jealous, pretending someone was flirting with me and those upsetting consequences. Now I think about the possibility that Nathan has slept with Brenna and the anger and vindictiveness stir up wildly inside of me all over again.

All my thoughts snarl together and sorting them out doesn't seem possible anymore. Ever. Can this be the definition of crazy? No, this is the definition of stress. I suddenly realize Nathan and my mother have it all wrong where I'm concerned. They've mixed up psychotic and unstable with confused and overwhelmed. Has anyone in my life ever really understood me? As I further mull over the perplexing feelings Ruth's writing arouses in me, someone lightly touches my shoulder. For the second time this evening, Sam has crept up behind me.

"You look confused and overwhelmed," Sam says, as if on cue. He kneels down and gently kisses me on the lips.

The alarming look on my face is possibly what stops him in his tracks and he apologizes for his impulsiveness. But he tells me to follow him into his den. I remember what happened before and I do not want to go back there. To his laboratory. The couch was his operating table, the sunlight his microscope and Sam's searing eyes, sharper than any surgical instrument, dissecting me inside and out. No, I don't want to go. But I sense I don't have much choice—Sam leads me decisively by the hand. He knows he punches my timecard now.

I find the den to be much safer at night than during the daytime. A fire crackles invitingly in the hearth and there are rumpled blankets on the formerly austere couch, as if someone recently spent a cozy night here. I crouch down by the flames and let my cheeks warm to the blaze.

"Nordis, the irony in this whole matter is that I was going to ask Ruth for a trial separation in the next couple of months."

What can I say to that? Ironic how? Because now they are separated for eternity? I feel a gust of air movement and can tell he kneels close behind me.

"What you just read is unfortunately how the beginning of the end happened for us. We were both on that website, apparently looking for the same thing. But you're only hearing her perspective. I'm not proud to admit I was looking to stray from my marital vows. But I had been very unhappy as well." He looks to me for acknowledgment and I nod.

"Having a baby was meant to be our glue. When I couldn't produce any paste so to speak," Sam reddens, "Ruth simply borrowed another adhesive. But by then, let's just say we found ourselves in a very sticky situation, pardon the pun." He smiles and I realize how outright handsome I find him.

"Oh," I look up at the ceiling. This is what I do when I'm feeling self-conscious. I've learned not to look down, because people follow your gaze with their own eyes and it's not a pretty view. Besides it exaggerates my double-chin.

I think about Ruth's "needs" as she described them in her story in conjunction with what Sam says just now. Was there really a medical, artificial-insemination between Sam's brother and Ruth, or did she conceive Caden the old-fashioned way? My heart goes out to Sam.

"Nordis, I'm very attracted to you. I was drawn to you from the first night you came to visit Ruth. I just feel terrible for our current plight," Sam says.

Our? In a day or so he'll be completely absolved and this will be my own personal hell. Mine. Concentrating on the choice of possessive pronouns is a lot easier than focusing on the meaning of his words. Or the fact that he's raking his fingers through my matted hair. A flurry of giddiness rises somewhere deep inside me. A flurry of giddiness or a giddy flurry? Which would be correct in an essay? Sam presses against me now, easing me backwards with the weight of his body. He strokes my shoulders underneath my blouse and I flinch, anticipating the pain and burning that usually follows someone assaulting my skin, but there is none.

The rug is soft beneath my thighs but I hope it's not one of those real animal skin carpets that people put next to fireplaces in mountain cabins. I used to be a vegetarian. My mind plays hopscotch. Is this really happening? Am I really letting Sam kiss me harder and deeper now so there's an urgency to his groans and his breath comes in deep exhales? Yes, I am. And now his fingers toy with the buttons on my top but I know I won't allow this to continue. This is different than the earlier clinical exam he gave me to rule out something horrible. This will lead to something horrible.

Even if I can get past Nathan and my marriage and everything else that plagues me, I am mortified that a man like Sam will see me without my strategically placed lingerie. My shield. With Nathan it's different. He's familiar with our darkened routine, the garments stay on, he doesn't gawk or touch me there and I'm the one who shifts into the positions I deem safe throughout our well choreographed lovemaking. Nathan knows the drill. (I actually hate when people say that.) But Nathan slept with Brenna.

Sam seems to be taking complete charge here. Part of me is pleased that he even has the desire to. The rest of me remains terrified at what he will uncover in his zeal. The Zeal Reveal. The Fervor Favor. The Concerning Yearning. The Passion Compassion. Sam feels sorry for me. Yes, that's it. This is pity passion. My eyes are closed and I concentrate on words, rhymes and metaphors—anything but this actual moment.

I hear little gasps and moans and recognize they are my own. Am I arching my back because I'm tense or to feel more of Sam, who is ravenous to feel more of me? I'm aware of him pressing against me with a huge immediacy as I feel his ever-increasing bulge below. It's fairly apparent how very much he wants me. But can that really be true? I open my eyes to see Sam looking at me desiring, not despising. Yes it can.

"You are a beautiful woman, Nordis," Sam interrupts my thoughts. "Let's give each other this one night." He fervently mashes his mouth into mine, his tongue exploring the edges of my lips. I'm intoxicated with his scent, recalling how earlier I couldn't predict if he was going to be forceful and aggressive or kind and gentle. I close my eyes again and finally relax and allow myself to experience these electrifying sensations fully. Has Nathan ever kissed me like this? Have I ever permitted Nathan to kiss me like this?

"You damn well have not!" Nathan barges in. My god, Nathan! I knew it. When I phoned home earlier tonight, the telephone was probably previously tapped and my call was traced. My conspiring mother-in-law no doubt reported immediately to her son the origin of the call. She could've easily given him this address. Oh my god.

"You see? One never knows what goes on behind closed doors!" I listen to my mother quoting. And I remember what she said after I had walked in on my first husband with that psychiatrist, "If one cannot resist temptation, one should avoid it."

There's something else I know I should be remembering right now. I frantically think back two years ago to Paul, my brother-in-law and his unexpected death. What did Nathan really do to him that night? An overdose, strangulation, suffocation perhaps? Those were quiet plans. But Nathan will have loud, deafening plans for tonight. I just know it. A noisy blast. And I can plainly see his gun.

Chapter 36

REMOVED

It's all in my mind's eye.

"This is wrong," I say breathily and bolt up to a sitting position again. I don't need Nathan or my mother intruding into my thoughts to know morality. Sam stops kissing me and nods an understanding okay. He angles his head until we're eye to eye. There's a palpable cooling off between us as we sever our embrace but I also notice the fireplace has died down to smoldering embers. Sam lowers me onto his chest, pushing my head to the side so my ear rests against his heart. He gently places his right hand over my own heart. We stay in this position for an hour, not speaking. In this way, I can listen to his heart but he touches mine.

When the telephone rings sharply, we both know who it will be.

"Come to the hospital," Brenna says. "Please."

We wake the housekeeper up and she seems traumatized to see both of us together but willingly offers to stay with my baby when she realizes we are leaving. On the drive over, Sam details much more about the genetic disorder called Trisomy. He explains that Trisomy 18 is called Edward's Syndrome. And that organ transplants will be a likely scenario with either Trisomy 18 or 13 but that will only buy time, nothing more. But he also fears Bridget is too small to survive any surgery and if she goes septic it will all be a moot point. I can't even bring myself to ask what septic is. I guess I haven't realized how attached I am to that little peanut girl. I instinctively look in the back seat but nobody is there, so all I can do is think gratefully about my own beautiful, healthy son. I wish I'd brought him with me instead of leaving him with Rosa.

Sam changes the subject and asks me a direct question. Is it that I really yearn for a daughter or do I just not want a son? This makes me think and wrestle with some difficult issues. It also makes me realize Sam is the first person who has not made me feel horrible for my feelings; he just wants to understand them better. I babble (probably disjointedly) about unfamiliarity with boys and what makes them tick, how certain males from my past have hurt and betrayed me terribly, how detached boys can be from their mothers, how sometimes I feel I'm raising future gang-members because they're so . . . I stop in mid sentence at this point and don't even bother finishing with the word violent. He realizes the irony and looks at me. We're both thinking about what I did to Ruth.

Sam tells me something I won't soon forget. He explains that anyone can become aggressive and it's not a male or female trait. It's a perspective. He tells me it's up to the individual to demonstrate their character, their essence, and their humanity through their actions. He clarifies for me that it's easy to become confused if you don't look beyond the facts. Imagine that a small child observes a knife brandished in the hands of a murderer, Sam continues on, and then the youngster views that same knife wielded in the hands of a competent surgeon. Will the little kid be able to tell the difference between the two events?

"Oh," I say, "You mean like how a man can use his penis to either make love to a woman or to rape her?" Sam stares at me for a very long time and almost swerves out of his lane.

At the hospital in the neonatal intensive care unit, people move quickly and I take it from Sam's grim expression, this isn't a good sign. A baby is in crisis.

We find Brenna crying into her hands in an isolated chair along a metal hallway. All at once, I curse both Nathan and myself (one of us is obviously responsible) for bringing this young girl here alone, away from her family and her support system back home. Sam and I stand on either side of her, each of us stroking her back. She looks up, saturated in tears. I start to cry too and realize I'm beside myself with what's happening. I need a little distance. I can feel the disconnection and the detachment descending upon me—I'm outside of it all, just an observer . . .

INTERIOR—HOSPITAL CORRIDOR—NIGHT

Metallic and sterile, nurses huddle together, then disperse like football players off to execute a complicated play.

CLOSE UP: BRENNA, red-eyed teenage girl who should be thinking about theorems and postulates, but instead thinks about respirators and transplants as she sits on a folding chair.

SAM, an astute doctor and NORDIS, a disheveled mother, look like they're together but not really, don't seem to know where to put their helpless hands.

BRENNA
I don't understand what's happening.
The nurses tell me I can't help my own
baby. They say my blood is all wrong.

Nordis strokes the young woman's hair and glances down the hallway. What she sees drains the color from her face. She grabs a side wall railing to steady herself.

Sam is unaware that Nordis is disturbed and walks away from the two women to get the real scoop from the supervising physician.

NORDIS
(shaky voice)
Sam will get to the bottom of this. Hold tight,
I'm here with you too. But Brenna, why didn't
you tell me Nathan was here at the hospital?

BRENNA
(sniffling)
That hotel maid told him which hospital we went to.
He's been talking to me so nicely, telling the hospital
man in charge he'll pay all the bills. Now he's going to
pick my mom up at the airport. I need my mother.

NORDIS
Of course you do.

Nordis watches the back of her husband, NATHAN, handsome ophthalmologist, mid-thirties, stride away. He gets smaller and smaller until he disappears completely out an emergency exit door and sets off the alarm.

Both women hold their ears to muffle the ringing.

Sam returns.

SAM
Sorry. Some clown set off security.

He crouches down at eye level with Brenna.

SAM
Bridget is septic. I'm trying to get you in there.
You have different blood types. It's complicated
and has to do with RH factors. It's not important
now though.

Sam hugs Brenna. She looks so young, a passerby could mistake her for Sam's granddaughter.

SAM
(To Nordis)
Can I talk to you over here?

Nordis moves a few feet away with Sam close by her side.

SAM
Nordis, there's maybe a few hours left. Maybe.

Nordis hugs Sam, burying her face in his shoulder.

SAM
I thought I understood you. More importantly,
I thought you were done lying to me.

Nordis cocks her head and looks quizzically at Sam.

SAM
If you had told me from the start that Brenna was
not the biological mother, time might've been saved
screening blood and organ transplants.

Nordis continues to stare, dazed.

NORDIS
(loudly)
What? What do you mean?

JUDITH, Nordis' mother, a well put together older woman, clicks toward them from a hallway in her dress pumps. She carries a styrofoam coffee cup, the kind that comes from a vending machine. Judith rushes her last few steps as she eyes her daughter's expression.

JUDITH
She was not supposed to find out like this.
Couldn't you have waited for her husband
to return? Or for me, her own mother? To tell her
that it's her baby.

Nordis buckles, collapses. Judith bends to comfort Nordis.

JUDITH
I know, I know, Nordis. But sometimes people do the wrong things for the right reasons. The most important thing is that we've found you and you're okay.

Chapter 37

SUCH A TOUCH

Nobody has the right to tell you what the most important thing is. Ensconced deep inside the neonatal ward, I stand next to Brenna, both of us dressed in sterile hospital suits and masks as we touch baby Bridget with our gloves through the small holes in her isolette. Sam stands between us, carefully monitoring the baby's vital signs.

I have a baby girl. I knew it all along. I have a daughter. I felt it in the delivery room all those weeks ago just the same as I feel it here now. I have a baby girl. And I won't allow anything to block me from seeing her, including my own tears. I swipe at my face madly, my sheathed fingers slicking salty drops to the floor as Sam looks at me. For the first time I see the corners of his eyes watering and I know this must be a sign. He's letting me know there isn't much time for all the mother-daughter things I've wanted to do and the talks I've always planned to have. I need to find another way. Sam helps me do that.

"At this point, it's okay to take off your gloves. You can feel your daughter," he says. I have a baby girl.

I peel off the purple latex and my fingers reach for what I've been reaching for forever. Bridget has a frail, silky wrist and her little fingers finally unclench and relax with our physical contact. Her tightly furrowed brows ease apart as I gently caress this sweet little girl whose skin is finer than the fanciest milled powder dust. This is a precious touch and I soon learn that it will be one of the final touches. I will never again think of touching and being touched in any terms except wondrous. I remember the little beaded baby bracelet in my purse and I slip it on her delicate wrist. "Ava Rose." but she is so still now. Sam takes a deep breath and nods slightly to me—she is gone.

"The hell if I get reprimanded," Sam says and opens the top of the glass isolette. "You should be able to hold her when you say goodbye. Both of you should."

My throat closes up on me and I can't seem to find any words but what I want to say is that the mommy who took care of her these past weeks needs to hold her first. All I can do is gesture toward Brenna. Sam understands, gives me the kindest smile and gingerly places the baby in Brenna's arms. Brenna hums, "You are my sunshine, my only sunshine," softly into the baby's ear. I watch a young mother say goodbye to her daughter and realize that was the purpose of my own trip here. To slowly, ease my way into letting go of the daughter I'll never have. I finally did that tonight.

I don't know what going into shock feels like but I imagine it's like a movie halting mid-frame, the sound slowly distorting into low-pitched garbled syllables, the picture warped and frozen on the screen in suspended animation. This is what happens to me when within a few hours, I'm surrounded by all the people who've hurt me. Brenna's mother flew in and stands remotely by herself. I recognize her from when she visited Brenna in the hospital. My mother of course, waits to talk to me and then there is Nathan who paces around the corridor.

Nathan.

But Sam is behind me and he's put on his hospital name badge so he looks pretty official. What he does next, I will be forever grateful for.

"Folks, I know there's a lot to discuss here but our responsibility is for the patient and to her next of kin. I'm going to kindly ask that all you well meaning people give these two ladies their time, respect, and privacy, as our hospital personnel assists them with their needs and helps them through their next steps. I know they will contact you when they are ready. Jeannie and Marsha will escort you to the lobby. Good night." Two uniformed nurses prod everyone away reluctantly.

Brenna, Sam and I stand together, not knowing what to do and where to go. Even though Sam appeared so professional just moments before, he now looks like someone whose routine has been turned inside-out. Brenna has fallen completely silent and a light within her seems to have dimmed. Sam tells us we can stay the night with him or we can stay in the hospital in a room on a different ward that he can authorize for us. Arrangements must be made of course, but they can be dealt with in the morning. I'm vaguely aware there's another baby that needs arrangements and to finally have a real name bestowed upon him.

Brenna and I opt to stay at the hospital and Sam leads the way to the surgical center where he tells us it will be far easier sleeping among women who will be having breast enhancements than women who will be breastfeeding. People stare at us as we walk by and it seems to me, they whisper as well.

I look at Sam to see if he understands what might be happening but his expression turns sour and I spy an important looking official, accompanied by a security guard tersely approaching our small group.

"Manning, in light of your current situation, your residency privileges have been permanently revoked at this institution. Please vacate the premises at once." This rude head official doesn't even wait until he's near us before he shoots out his words.

I pull Brenna by the arm and pretend to point out a painting on the wall, talking to her about it in hushed tones. I've learned long ago that the way to preserve someone's dignity when they've just been humiliated is to pretend you haven't just witnessed it. That's definitely a time when a lie helps someone.

When Sam finally takes a few steps toward us, he doesn't appear to be his normal six foot height. I speak before he can.

"Sam, the beds here look just lousy. I think Brenna and I want to go to your house, if that's okay?"

Sam's eyes are the kindest I've ever seen them.

Back at Sam's house, Brenna and I both look in on the sleeping baby. Rosa has obviously given him a feeding because I observe the empty bottle of formula on the night table. I look in the crib at this sleeping cherub and note his hair is starting to come in a bit. And it's dark, like Brenna's, not red like mine. There are thoughts in the back of my head that I stuff way, way down. I brush my lips to his forehead. It's late and I don't know anything anymore. Brenna and I hug goodnight and I briefly wonder where Sam went.

During the night, I have a vivid, lucid dream. It's not convoluted or complicated and I can easily articulate it without confusion.

I am at a water park with Nathan, the boys and little Ava Rose. We are enjoying the day and the sound of happy, splashing laughter permeates the air. Just then a distraught teenage girl rushes up to me, her eyes wild with panic.

"Can you help me? Someone has taken my baby. I just closed my eyes for a minute and when I opened them, she was missing from my towel."

I jump up to assist this poor hysterical girl and she describes her baby in great detail, emphasizing she wears a bright, pink one-piece suit. I search everywhere I can think of, especially at the bottom of the swimming pool and in the restrooms as well. When I come out of the bathroom, the teenage girl is nowhere to be found and I pray hard that she's been united with her little girl. When I return to my own family, Nathan calmly tells me someone just snatched Ava Rose. He turned around to sunscreen the boys and when he looked back, she was gone.

"Nooo," I scream and break into a frenzied run to the closest woman who sits on a lounge chair. She's just a few yards away, yet it takes me forever to reach her. She holds her baby on her lap and vigorously bounces her knees while singing "The Noble Duke of York."

"Please, can you help me? Someone has run off with my baby girl. Please help me search for her!"

The woman stops her song and grasps her baby tighter. She gives me an unkind look, malicious even, before she replies.

"I've heard all about this ploy. Asking someone to help you with your "missing" child and then when they try to assist you, you steal their own baby. Shame on you."

Chapter 38

PAST, PRESENT, AND FUTURE TENSE

I must cry out in my sleep during this dream because suddenly Sam hovers over me making soothing sounds and patting me on the back. I used to think that was so romantic, screaming from a nightmare and having the man who cares about you fly to your side and rescue you from your unconscious demons. I think I saw Rhett Butler do this once with Scarlett O'Hara in a movie. Sometimes I used to purposely whimper around midnight and toss wildly about, but Nathan was a sound sleeper and never woke up. But now Sam has come running to reassure me it's only a nightmare. My body is soaked with perspiration, my hair sticks up at strange angles and my breath is probably sickening. The experience is not at all what I fantasized it would be.

As I assimilate back into reality from the bizarre dreamlike consciousness, I can hear it's raining hard outside and the drops pounding on the metal roof make a tinny sound. Sam tells me he'll be right back and out of habit, I jump up to quickly rinse my mouth. When he returns he has donuts and hot cocoa on a tray. I express surprise and tell Sam that I haven't had this combination of donuts and hot cocoa since I was five years old. With my father.

I reminisce aloud how my father used to come home from work and if it was raining out, a rare event in Southern California, but if it was, he would scoop me up in my footed jammies and load me up into his station wagon. Not my brother, just me. On the way to Winchell's donut shop, he would tell me the names of different cars and I would always point to Volkswagen Bugs. My father told me that was a bad car built by a very mean man and if you looked at the front head-on you could even see the awful man's face. When we arrived at the donut shop, my father would carry me in his arms so I wouldn't get my pajama feet wet in the parking lot. I'll never forget how the donut shop owner and any lingering customers would stare approvingly and remark how sweet it was to see a father and his daughter on their own special date.

Watching me balance the steaming cup of hot chocolate between my chubby little hands and simultaneously lick the glazed sugar off the donut with my tongue was something my dad always chuckled over. That's when he would tell me to have a daughter of my own when I grew up so when I got too old to do this anymore, he would have another little girl to take out to a donut shop. And you should name her Rose, he'd insist and I knew that was after his little sister who had perished in the holocaust but nobody liked to talk about that.

"I'll never be too old for this, Daddy," I'd say. "Rose. That's a name for flowers." I used to pronounce that last word with a funny lisp because "fl" blends were still hard for me at that age.

"Promise me you'll use Rose as a middle name then. For your daughter, Nordie," he'd say. "Because your mother wouldn't let me use it for you." I'd promise happily, glad it wasn't too hard to get my father's approval.

Sam encourages me to tell him more about my Dad and I wonder why he wants to hear stuff like this, especially now. But I go on.

It did get a little harder to get my father's approval in school because I wasn't very good at math. "Math is about numbers and numbers are money and money keeps you safe," my father used to say (his own original quote) and so I'd try extra hard to get A's in arithmetic even though I had to cheat and copy Sonya's paper sometimes. My mother would hover nearby and put in her own two cents, "Money doesn't buy happiness."

My father also adored my writing and I made it a point to write stories about him during free period in school. Sometimes if there wasn't time in class, I would stay in at recess working devotedly to finish a new tale. When he came home late from work, I was permitted to stay up to read aloud to him the stories about the zany character named Max. My father would snicker and hoot hysterically, then ruffle my hair.

"Promise me one day Nordis, you'll publish these Max stories," he'd say. "So the poor fellow can live on forever." I promise, Daddy.

I wed my first husband, the Jewish engineer, because it made my father so proud to have me marry within our faith. But my Dad's nuptial happiness was nothing compared to the outburst of jubilation he displayed when I gave birth to my first baby and named him Michael, for my father's own father, who also died in the war. Everything was blissful and idyllic until the eighth day when it was time for the circumcision ceremony to take place.

Traditionally it's the grandfather who holds the newborn on a special pillow on his lap during the traditional cutting of the foreskin. As I watched my father stoically gripping the satin cushion, I noticed that he wouldn't look down, only straight ahead, his eyes seemingly locked on a sepia toned, intergenerational family photograph on our wall. After the bleeding and the horrifying cries of my baby echoed around the room, my father jumped up abruptly and handed me the pillow with little Michael still squirming on it. I watched sadly as he bolted from the room.

"Must bring back bad memories for him," I heard a few relatives murmur. "It did sound like the poor little guy was being tortured."

My dad came downstairs hours later and apologized. "He's a wonderful little boy. But work on that girl next," he reminded me. "A little granddaughter for me to spoil and indulge. And don't forget about the name Rose, we had a deal," he'd wink. But there was no daughter to follow and ten years later I got divorced. And my father seemed to forget how to wink.

He accepted my second marriage to Nathan; even though he wasn't Jewish, he deemed him affable enough. Acceptance wasn't the same as getting my father's approval though. But at least he didn't disapprove because I could never handle that from him. He joined us in welcoming the twin boys into the world but recognized the extreme disappointment on my part.

"Don't worry," he said. "You'll get the girl next time. I put in an order myself with the big guy upstairs. Be patient."

On the twin's first birthday, we all went out to a celebratory dinner, with my mother choosing a brand new, all-you-can-eat restaurant called, "*Sir Lancelot's Royal Buffet.*" I was apprehensive because I knew growing up that my father refused to eat at buffets or cafeterias, basically anywhere he was forced to stand in line to get food. My parents always had to avoid them in Las Vegas hotels. When I raised my concern about her choice of eateries, my mother wouldn't back down.

"Oh, that's absurd," she asserted. "It's not always about him. A selfish man wrapped up in himself makes a very small bundle," she said. "He needs to get over himself." I actually hate when people say that.

"Well, okay," I had reluctantly acquiesced because my eldest was begging to go somewhere where he could make his own ice-cream sundae.

"That's cute," Sam interrupts. "I love those sundae bars with the sprinkles. Sorry, go on." He reaches over to cover my shoulders with the blankets.

I tell Sam I need to stop here—I can't continue with the rest of the story. But he senses I need to, that it's important, and promises he'll sit next to me while we experience it together.

INTERIOR—SIR LANCELOT'S ROYAL BUFFET—DINNER TIME

Customers fidget impatiently in line, waiting for their turn to pay the cashier and begin their feast. Harsh, unflattering light from above casts a greenish color onto their skin.

MAX, Nordis' normally jovial father, lingers behind the rest of his family in line as he examines a knight's suit of armor displayed by the entry door. He speaks in soft tones to a young GIRL behind him in line but his words are not distinguishable.

Unexpectedly, Max reaches out and firmly pinches the young girl's cheeks. She cries out in pain, snapping her mother to attention, who attempts to slap Max but misses his face.

NORDIS, dressed casually, rushes to her father's side, mumbling profuse apologies to the woman and her daughter. She ushers her father away by the arm back to the part of the line where their own family congregates.

NORDIS
(Apprehensively)
Dad, what's happening?

Max looks around, distrustful.

MAX
You've got to make the cheeks look rosy
and healthy. So she won't get selected.

Nordis hugs her father tenderly then pushes past him, bypassing her mother, JUDITH, who tries to quiet a fussy twin baby in her arms. Nordis, in an attempt to reach her husband expediently, steps clumsily over a carseat on the floor which jostles JUSTIN, the other twin, who begins to scream, red faced. NATHAN stands unaware, in a three piece business suit, at the head of the line.

Nordis intends to warn Nathan that something serious has happened.

But it's too late. The restless crowd standing in line inside that claustrophobic castle lobby begins to clamor, shout, and use frightful language.

FEMALE CUSTOMER
Oh my god. Stop! Stop him!

Hearing the tumult, Nordis turns in time to see her father Max cup his hand firmly over baby Justin's nose and mouth and apply pressure. He starts to smother the screaming baby.

A man wrestles Max away from the frightened toddler.

CLOSE UP: Max's confused expression.

PAN TO: Nordis' look of horror.

DISSOLVE TO: Tears

Chapter 39

PREDICTIONS

Whether Sam detects that I can't continue discussing this any longer or whether he's just tired himself, he lets me stop relaying my story at this point. I think about talking just a few more minutes about the situation. Perhaps I should mention the doctors told me that my father's type of psychotic break with reality might have a hereditary factor to it? But then I think that wouldn't be important for Sam to know. He wouldn't even care.

Sam asks if I want him to lie next to me in bed since it's still dark out and I do. I very much want him near me but not really in a sexual sort of way. It's just that I feel a need to cuddle now. It's probably not just with Sam that I feel this way, probably lots of people I care about, I wouldn't mind cuddling with at this point. Somehow, it doesn't feel suffocating anymore.

We talk a little longer—the drowsy, early morning, intimate chatter two people who are instinctively familiar with one another, easily exchange. I tell him about my preggo poetry and he laughs. He tells me about a woman who gets her breasts enlarged and reduced for each new husband. I even tell him how I see the numbers 11:11 on the clock all the time and elsewhere too. That gives him pause and he grins but soon after, we both fall silent, probably thinking about the past and the future. But right now, it's nice to stay in the present.

In a few moments, with his arm slung over my waist, I can tell by his deep, cadenced breathing that Sam has drifted to sleep. I wonder if he was repulsed by my huge middle. He snores pretty loudly but I would never embarrass him by mentioning this. My father used to snore and my mother made a really big deal out of it, often announcing in front of company that she had to sleep in our guest room many nights. She finally went out and purchased earplugs and that seemed to solve her problem.

I speculate whether the roommate who now shares a room with my father wears earplugs too. I think of my Dad and softly cry because he would've loved to meet Ava Rose. But that's not possible now. A few months ago, when my father heard the results of my ultrasound and that I was finally having a little girl; he was thrilled and made a prediction she would forever change my life.

We had hatched our brilliant scheme one rainy morning over a cup of hot-chocolate. Institutional hot cocoa really leaves a lot to be desired, but it was still a cozy meeting. Only the donuts were missing. We needed a plan because little children were not allowed in his facility, due to the fact that some of the patients were prone to shouting out horribly inappropriate things at random. I wasn't afraid to visit though because I knew it was just the medication talking. When you know about these kinds of drugs, you can prepare yourself for what to expect from a loved one. And you can avoid taking these kinds of pills yourself, at all costs. But for my father, it was a different story and I can see how the drugs help him stay calm and clear-headed.

But the real reason that small children are not allowed on that kind of ward is that it is deemed dangerous for them. Some of the male patients have violent histories. I'm sure they classify my father in this same category on account of what he started to do to little Justin at that buffet. But that's just absolute garbage. I explained numerous times to the hospital chief-of-staff about my father's past. How his family and others were concealed in the basement of their neighbor's house part of their time in Poland during the war. And how if a little baby wouldn't stop crying, it could give their hiding place away, putting everyone in grave jeopardy. So the baby had to be silenced. This was important. For the greater good of all. My god, that kind of sounds like something my mother would say.

Anyhow, because my Dad was deemed a physical threat to others, he couldn't have any visiting passes to come off the ward. But our plan would've worked perfectly. We decided that I would tell the check-in nurses at the front that my due date was really two weeks later than it actually was. That way, I could give birth to my daughter; still have time to recover, and then sneak Ava Rose inside my zipped-up jacket on my next visit, looking justifiably pregnant. My dad and I had laughed at the cleverness of it all.

"Write that up in a Max story," he had said. And I will.

But right now, I listen to Sam softly snore and think about the day ahead. Soon this entire ordeal will all be over. It will come to its own inevitable conclusion. I will see Nathan and my mother and try to comprehend why they did what they did to me. But none of it will matter because I will tell them that the day after tomorrow, I'm turning myself in to the police for homicide.

After that, I'm sure it will be my turn to do all the explaining.

Sam's breathing lightens up and he turns to me.

"Nordis?"

"Yes?" I ask, wondering how some people can wake up so quickly without needing to shake off a certain fuzzy grogginess.

"Brenna told me last night that she wants you to keep the baby. She thinks you're a wonderful, loving and experienced mother."

Will I ever get used to the sudden bulging in my throat that thoroughly impedes my speech? Momentarily unable to talk, I think about this baby boy that I have come to truly love with all my heart during our past week together. I can't bear the thought of abandoning him while I'm incarcerated for god knows how long. The baby should be with his rightful mother. That is the right thing to do. I try to explain all this to Sam, but there's too much weeping and stammering and hesitations and I can't tell if he gets what I'm saying. After he speaks, I realize this will be the last time I will ever wonder if Sam truly "gets me."

"You will raise this baby," Sam says with the force of someone who makes a prediction they are certain of. "And your other children at home too. You will continue to visit your father, make amends with your mother and welcome your eldest home from rehab. You will finally let your husband really look at you. And you will write a story about all this one day. Because you will not go to prison."

Chapter 40

THE MISSING "PEACE"

I feel as if I'm waiting for the missing piece of a puzzle to be revealed but so far nothing makes any sense. I sit and listen to my mother, Brenna's mother (Barbara) and Nathan all talk, well sort of, at the same time to Brenna and me. But it actually does begin to add up in a strange way which, if you really understand my family and all the past demented dynamics, is about the only way it inevitably can. Someday I will explain in more detail. Meanwhile, I ask a question of my mother.

"So when you were in Brenna's house and she refused your adoption idea, is that when you thought of just switching babies?"

"Oh no, Nordis," she says defensively. "That suggestion came from Barbara here. She kept my phone number and called me later that week with her own new idea." I'm dubious that there are other mothers out there as controlling as mine, but I fix my eyes coldly on Brenna's mother, Barbara.

Barbara shifts uncomfortably in her seat and rubs her thigh against the leather upholstery which emits an embarrassing sound.

"Oh dear," Barbara blushes. "You see, Brenna has this whole future ahead of her. I knew she'd thank me later for coming up with a guilt-free way for her to have her freedom back."

"Just remember that sometimes people do the wrong things for the right reasons," my mother interjects.

"You've already said that, Mom" I say. "And it's bullshit. I want to hear from Barbara now." I turn back to Brenna's mother expectantly. But Barbara demurely looks at her shoes and my mother seizes the gap.

"Nordis, I love you and couldn't bear for you to be disappointed and grieving over a baby girl with all kinds of fatal birth defects," my mother who can't seem to manage sharing a dialogue continues. "You had other children at home and frankly I wasn't sure, in your already fragile state, if it would put you over the edge." She hesitates, but not for long. "Nathan and I figured it was better for you to have a healthy baby boy than a stillborn baby girl. We did try to have Dr. Grant find someone carrying a girl that was due around the same timeframe, but it just wasn't possible. Brenna's mother persuaded us she was the right candidate and I know she felt she was truly doing what was best for her daughter. Just as we were convinced we were doing the correct thing for you. Sometimes you just have to be cruel to be kind." By the end of this long speech, her voice has climbed several octaves.

Nathan interrupts and for once I'm grateful he does. This is one time when hearing his level-headed, non-emotional voice will help me.

"Nordie, nobody expected her to live for even an hour. Dr. Grant called me the day of our fateful ultrasound and told me what he saw on that screen would be terminal from the start. The poor thing." Nathan stops and looks genuinely broken up. "He advised me to prepare you for a late-term abortion but I knew you better than that."

At least Nathan had that part right. Dr. Grant! I had forgotten about his involvement in this thing. But of course being that Nathan works in the same building and they are professional colleagues and all. Wasn't this illegal? Couldn't Dr. Grant get in tremendous trouble? I'm guessing some major money crossed hands here. And probably for Barbara too. I look at her and think about trips to Paris and new wardrobes.

Nathan persists that since Brenna was a minor, her mother was able to make a decision on her behalf to give the baby up. I am doubting this answer but I let Nathan continue with his rationalization. The problems started, Nathan explains, when at the last minute, Brenna refused a general anesthesia for her C-section. I look at Brenna at this point in the conversation and she nods to confirm this statement.

"Since she chose to have a local spinal tap instead of going totally under, she was awake when her son was born and heard his healthy cries. At that point, there was no choice," Nathan emphasizes. "And they had to whisk her son out of the room before she saw him. This was done under the pretense of bathing him, and in a few moments, the nurse returned with a cleaned up, miracle baby girl. Meanwhile, the little guy was brought to our delivery room." Nathan looks at the inside of his palm like a nervous boy who has pre-written notes for a pop quiz.

I think back to this time period but it all seems a hazy blur, given that I was in shock. But it occurs to me that must be why postpartum, the snippy nurses all discouraged me from walking around the maternity ward. I remember how I had wandered into Brenna's room and that one head nurse was positively rude.

"So you never knew if you were having a boy or a girl?" I ask Brenna directly, still trying to sort this out in my own mind.

She shakes her head. "I wanted to be surprised."

"Well, I guess we both were," I say. I mean it as sort of a sarcastic, cavalier remark but suddenly the tears spring and I'm weeping uncontrollably for the umpteenth time in twenty-four hours. And the anger isn't far behind. "Why couldn't you just let me have my baby girl right from the start?" I rail at everyone and at no one. "Why couldn't you let me have . . . my life?"

Nathan and my mother hang their heads. If I look intently, I can see the small tremors in my mother's hands and also in this position, the prominent gray hair is also visible where her roots are growing out. She's getting on in years. Do I really want to have an ongoing vendetta with her? And Nathan. Right now he looks like a man who can't figure anything out. As smart a man as he is, with all his textbook knowledge, that feeling must frustrate him to no end. I look at them both long and hard and they seem truly remorseful.

Are you supposed to hold people accountable when they commit abhorrent deeds under the strong conviction that they're acting honorably? I think back to Sam's analogy with his knife. If a surgeon tries to do good, but the surgery ends up botched, is the surgeon now culpable?

I'm frightened because somehow this situation seems similar to when I tried to make Nathan jealous. At the time, it was because I wanted to elicit passion from him in the hopes of strengthening our marriage. That was a positive goal but with disastrous consequences. I ponder this more as I remember the horrible events that must've unfolded at my sister-in-law's home that particular night. "Be careful what you wish for," I hear my mother articulate.

Did she actually just say that? I look up, but no, both of their heads are still bowed down in despair and repentance. I focus on them, close my eyes and when I reopen them, I make the decision to forgive. For their sake, for Ava Rose's sake, for Brenna's sake, and as a tribute to Sam.

Chapter 41

GUTTER GROWN GARDENIAS

I feel surreal. I am in a hotel room with my own husband, we've been married for six years and I don't have the slightest idea what to talk about when he comes out. Nathan is in the shower, cleaning up, and then we're expected to go to the funeral. I've dressed myself in a simple black skirt that I had to run out and buy. Of course I hadn't brought any clothing like this from home. Who packs just in case there's a funeral to attend?

Perhaps I should use this hotel computer just one last time. But for what? Would I log into *The Rare Affair* website and browse? What if I run into an ad for Nathan there? I smile at the irony of that. I check my email instead and surprisingly there is one lone letter. It is from Jane.

>*Dear Author Nordis,*
>
>*Congratulations! Your latest story has been accepted for publication.*
>
>>*Jane*
>>*Editor-in-Chief*
>>*Gratitude Magazine*

I have finally been accepted. I have a feeling this is the first of many times Jane will help me feel acceptable. But who is Jane really? Before I can contemplate the implications further, the hotel phone on my bed table rings louder than it ever has. It is the exact time Nathan's mother is supposed to call and I have rehearsed everything.

"Hi Silvia. I want to thank you so much for helping out with the boys. Do you think I can say hello to whichever twin is nearby?" Please just hand the phone over woman, I think as I cram down the rest of a Hostess cupcake.

"Nordis? Is that you? Nordis, what is going on? Nathan tells me so little. I know you've been under a lot of tension dear, but have you tried taking your medication?" I absolutely cannot respond to this.

"Everyone takes a little something now and then, Nordis," she continues, "it's nothing to be ashamed of. Dressing a boy as a girl will lead to disastrous consequences later in life. Didn't anyone ever tell you that? And they certainly make a lot of nice pant suits nowadays," she pauses. Oh my god. In her head, I am the problem. Does she even have an inkling what her son has done?

"Silvia, may I just talk to one or both of my children please?"

"Dear, they're napping now."

"Five year olds don't need naps," I say spacing my words nice and evenly. "They need to go swimming."

"I don't get my hair wet, Nordis. Besides the news has just come on and it's very exciting. The daughter of the owner of Fuji's dress shop has been arrested for prostitution. She's been wearing clothing from his store and he looks deeply ashamed. I'll have them phone you later." Click.

Shame. Shame and respect. I think of my father. I touch my own hair and decide to try on a bathing suit when I return home. The boys need to go swimming. I turn on the television to look for the Fuji dress shop story but remember that I won't pick up Los Angeles news. As I switch channels, I drop the remote and freeze. Sam.

". . . And local authorities say the prominent Colorado breast surgeon admitted to committing the grizzly crime late this afternoon but due to his longstanding position in the local community, is being released on his own recognizance. He will await indictment under Supreme Court arraignment in the same Boulder home he has shared with his late wife of seventeen years. Dr. Samuel Manning, when questioned about his sudden and spontaneous confession, had only this to say . . ."

"Sometimes people do the right thing for the wrong reason." Sam's distinguished face looks off to the side. And then he is gone. In a coming-up-next preview, little children are shown playing dodge ball on a city street, the camera focuses on flowers sprouting up from the cracks of sidewalks and the dirty street gutters. Gardenias growing in gutters. All in all, the clearing in local winter weather is hailed as a major celebration—apparently the sun is finally coming out in this part of the country.

I turn around and see Nathan leaning partially naked in the bathroom doorway, his handsome figure silhouetted by the lights in the background. This is the first time I've seen him without a suit in a long time. How long has he been standing there?

"What a bastard, killing his own wife in cold blood," Nathan comments. I suck in my breath and am just grateful Nathan hasn't put it together that he saw Sam yesterday in the hospital.

"Nathan, I have to go down to the lobby. I need to buy nylons from the gift shop," I say and I'm almost out the door before my last words are pronounced. My god, what has Sam done! What does that mean, the right thing for the wrong reason? Hadn't my mother said just the opposite? She said they did the wrong thing for the right reason? I am so mixed up; the only thing I know is that I must phone Sam.

The payphone is occupied with a breathtakingly beautiful, model-type woman. Black mascara tears stream down her cheeks as her shaking hand clutches a pregnancy test box. This is Audrey I realize, and make a respectful decision to pretend I haven't seen her. I duck back and hide around the gift shop corner, covering my ears so as not to eavesdrop on her conversation. When it's finally my turn, the phone is still damp.

My heart flutters as he answers on the first ring. "Hello Nordis," Sam says smoothly. How does he know it's me? But then I realize this must show up on his caller identification system as my hotel payphone number.

"Sam, No! You can't do this," I say plaintively. Suddenly I wish I had gone to see him in person. But there's Nathan, there's my baby, there's a funeral, and there's respect and honor. "What are you thinking?" I ask instead.

"I'm thinking of you." This stops me for a minute.

"You can't take the rap for me," I say and dampen the receiver further with my own tears.

"Nordis, you have everything to live for . . . your children, all four of them now, your marriage, your friendship with Brenna, who will need you very much by the way. Watching over your father, making peace with your mother and your wonderful imagination. I'm older and my career has run its course. I can do this. Let me do this."

"Sam, what is the right thing for the wrong reason?"

"The right thing is to confess. The wrong reason is . . ."

"Sam? Sam?" I think the line has gone dead.

"I'm here. The wrong reason is because I've fallen in love with you."

Chapter 42

NOISES OFF

The man who sits in front of me on the plane ride back to Los Angeles has long, shaggy hair and I think that he needs a good trim. I look at Nathan holding baby Charlie, both of them doze next to me, twitching every so often, as if they share the same dream. I wonder how they can both relax enough to sleep when the engine on the plane sounds like a ratcheting chain saw. I think about a time long ago when my hearing played tricks like this on me once before.

It used to happen a lot at the beauty salon where I worked during college. My hearing would become heightened. By that, I mean fine tuned, really sharp and I wouldn't miss a sound. I think it was a side effect of this new antidepressant my mother had me on at the time. That was yet another occasion when she deemed me depressed because I was sleeping a lot more than she thought I should. My ears were so acute that I could even hear the sound people's hair made and it got to be sort of a guessing game, figuring out the noise it would make when I cut it.

I remember I had told Ruth about it and she laughed (which sounded like a xylophone) as we both styled countless, cranky customers with our stations directly across from one another, on those long, hot summer afternoons during our last quarter before graduation.

Curly hair was by far the easiest to guess. It almost always made a wire-like noise when you snipped it, kind of like a Slinky. Red hair could sizzle like bacon frying or even make an abrupt snapping sound like when a carrot is bitten. Brown hair was a little trickier to guess because it varied, depending on the shade. Dark brown was like the noise windshield wipers made when you turned them on without rain. Light brown was tinfoil being ripped on that serrated edge thingy.

But the highlighted blondes were the sneaky ones, complete wild cards. By that I mean, their hair sometimes didn't make any sound at all. But it wasn't really silent, either. Not really.

Most days, Ruth and I would lessen our boredom by having a little friendly competition. Who could get the most drop-ins, by request? Those were the customers who just spontaneously came in without an appointment. I can't imagine strolling down the street and having a sudden craving for a haircut, but many people did just that.

It wasn't really a fair contest because Ruth had quite a client following and she was always heavily requested. I know what she did to deserve that too. As she'd cut a male client's hair, she always made sure to lean in close enough so that her pert breasts would "accidentally" brush against some part of his body. Additionally, if he was wearing a tank top or short sleeve shirt, she would often let her highlighted blonde, silky hair sweep sensuously across his shoulders or arms. Ruth kept careful track of her customer's appreciative expressions by watching the whole scenario in the mirror. I never looked in the mirror when I worked because I hated to see my own reflection. But that whole repertoire of hers earned Ruth quite a lot of tips and referrals, which she also kept careful track of.

On this one particular day, my first customer had greasy, gray hair and it threw me off completely with the noise. It sort of tinkled like the bell over the salon shop door. Or maybe that actually was the bell jingling because lots of people filed inside and the waiting room filled to capacity as I began to perspire profusely under the fluorescent lights.

I had this elderly gentleman anchored down in my chair with a heavy gray robe, like they make you wear for an x-ray. I always wondered what kind of sound the robe would make if you dropped it. Probably crashing cymbals. I made good-humored small talk with him. I was always skilled at conversing with old people on account of my grandmother living with us. I held the scissors exactly like I'd been trained, on a slant, and was just about to trim his crown when I saw it. Dandruff. I've always had a queasy stomach and sickened pretty easily, so I usually closed my eyes when that happened. But I kept up my cheerful banter so he wouldn't think anything was the matter.

I opened my startled eyes when I heard this tremendous clattering, like pots and pans clanging together and realized that my customer had jumped from his chair and thrown the gray robe onto the floor.

"I said just a little off the top!" His voice rose in crescendo.

It didn't take Ruth long to arrive at my side and I was relieved. She could always be counted on at times like that. With irate and irrational customers.

"Sir, let me take you in my station and fix that right up for you. She's not been feeling well lately." Then she shot me a "get it together" look.

"She wasn't even watching what she was doing," he grumbled.

It was the mirror that did me in. That was the one bad part of that job. Even when you thought you were behind someone's back, you really weren't.

After that incident I informed Ruth that I was taking a break in the back room. All the stylists seemed to be using their blow dryers and frankly the noise and the heat was starting to get to me. I was tired from carrying fifteen credits in college which was more than a full-time load. I lived at home to save money and my mother would rouse me at six am even though my first class wasn't until seven o'clock. At night.

"Rise and shine," she would say and jerk open my curtains so the bright sun would gush into my bed. "Lose an hour in the morning and you'll be all day hunting for it."

As I sat in the break room that day, I did a quick assessment of my life, which I often did periodically at that age. I had just gotten engaged to my first husband but something didn't feel quite right. Despite my hesitant feelings, I kept quiet because the whole family was finally excited over something I did. Nordis' personal accomplishment! She managed to get engaged, and to a Jewish engineer too. This glorious achievement warranted lots of parties. And a huge wedding was already in the works. My mother was a frustrated party planner and I spied the beginnings of a centerpiece being assembled in our garage, complete with glittered doves and Styrofoam hearts. And then there was my father.

I thought about my father's beaming face over my impending marriage. I couldn't back out now. Once again, I silently thanked whoever was responsible that he never found out about my shoplifting crime which had transpired just a few months prior to this time. I honestly don't know what I would've done if he had been called.

As I came out of the break room, I blinked my eyes to adjust to the bright salon lights and I remember being stupefied to see the handsome man reclined in Ruth's chair; his loosely coiled hair snip, snip snipped (a shuffling deck of cards sound) as he laughed heartily. It was my father!

"Oh, hello Nordie doll," he said brightly. "Ruth said you had gone home. Your mother nagged me in here to get a haircut before your engagement party."

"Oh, Max, you're so funny," Ruth laughed, the notes high on the xylophone scale. When did she start calling him by his first name?

Before I could say anything, the receptionist sent back another customer to my station—a teenage boy. He had dirty arms, a pierced ear and he chomped a thick wad of gum. Each pop of his bubble rang out like shots from a cannon. His request for a mohawk hairstyle frightened me because I had never done one before.

I didn't even bother trying to chit-chat with this kid. What could I possibly say that he would be interested in? Instead, I listened to the conversation between my father and Ruth. With my hearing so keen that day, I picked-up every word. I could also see her pressing against my father as she worked on his hair.

The next thing I overheard was Ruth remarking that I had already lost seven pounds on my new diet and wasn't my father proud? By the time the wedding rolled around, my dress would need to be taken in, she giggled flirtatiously. If I wanted my father to know these details, I would've told him myself, I thought. Then Ruth moved on to ask if my dad was going to wear a tuxedo and described her own formal dress. How could she possibly think my father could be interested in . . . suddenly my ears went on alert when I heard her mention Fuji's dress shop.

"It's such a shame Nordis has been banned from that store."

"Why is that?" my father inquired.

"Oops, I thought you knew about that unfortunate . . ." Ruth continued talking.

My ears throbbed as I hastily stretched out my arm in front of the punky boy to reach for a shiny object on the shelf, careful not to let my ever-protruding bust line come into contact with his tattooed shoulder.

"Hey, you don't use scissors with a mohawk!" the kid griped. But I didn't care. I just kept wondering, when was the last time Ruth had a haircut? When? When? When?

I was aware of people watching and then there was a horrible grating noise like the sound of ice cubes grinding in a blender and when I looked down, I had a thick hank of Ruth's shiny, blonde hair in my hands. She had been long overdue.

Chapter 43

THE SHALLOW END

Home. I am home. The first three months I've been back, I've moved as if in slow motion; like someone who is underwater. Today I decide I may as well go below the surface and so I fill our oversized oval bathtub. Usually I take showers. After sitting in the bath for a while, I remove my left contact lens and gently place it on the little ripples on top of the water. I watch it drift gradually down the drain. It doesn't go directly down, sort of spirals and meanders its way slowly along until it gets close enough that the sheer strength of the suction funnel slurps it down for good. There was definitely time to snatch it back up but I chose to let it go. These are the new contacts that Nathan recently fitted me with and they're tinted blue because I thought my brown eyes were boring.

I fill the tub back up with warmer water and close the drain again. I'm going on my fourth hour of soaking in this bathroom and still nobody has come knocking to check on me. I think about Sam. Would he have worried about me by now?

Sam is probably worrying about other things right now. I still can't believe that, in spite of the fact that I just met him, I let him know me better than people I've known my entire life. Or perhaps it was because of the fact that I had just met him. After all, what did I have to lose? I think of all the things Sam had to lose—his wife, his son, his career, and his freedom. Does he consider me to be a loss as well? I think that he does. But then I realize that I consider him a gain, a tremendous gain. I gained so much from his presence in my life. Perhaps there's something he feels I brought to his life too but probably not. There isn't a deadline for these kinds of things. I can still impart something meaningful to him and I think I will do it by writing him a story. A love story.

I hear giggling outside the bathroom door and consider my children. My baby Charlie (who now has a middle name suggested by Jane, 'Emmet,' which means truth) has learned to applaud and this is a very good thing. Jane actually taught him how to do it. She said I needed a number one fan that showed his passion. I am the only one he'll clap his little hands for, and I'm secretly thrilled about that. He gives a little round of applause when I pick him up, when I make funny faces and when I serve him food. It's utterly charming but inside I know it's just developmentally appropriate behavior at this point. But still, when he does it, there's a certain delight that emanates from inside his smile, joining everything and everyone around him together with his enchantment.

There is one other occasion when he puts his little hands together with enthusiasm and it's especially nice for me to observe—at the ballet. His eyes shine with glee at the graceful movements and the rapturous music. I don't care if people consider a ballet to be girly. We're planning a teddy bear tea-party next. I'm sure he'll still excel at Karate too. But the Karate will be used to protect or defend himself or a loved one (maybe me one day) from violence. It will not be used to promote violence.

Tomorrow Brenna will come over and we'll have a BBQ in the backyard, the weather will be lovely for a day of fun and food. You certainly can't have a BBQ in the rain. I will be introducing Brenna to my eldest son, Michael, who is coming home for a nice, long, two week trial visit. Depending how things go, he might stay with us forever or at least until he goes to college. Brenna bought me a new top with quarter length sleeves. I told her I would try wearing it tomorrow and if it feels okay, next time I'll even go sleeveless. Guess what? Brenna is a dancer! It is her that Charlie and I go and watch every weekend when she performs ballet at the Starlight Amphitheater. Afterwards, the three of us go out for ice-cream. I eat the ice-cream slowly and with glee, not guilt. Sometimes we even invite both our mothers to join us.

I'm going on six hours in this bath and I'm not sure why Nathan hasn't come looking for me yet. Any minute and he'll come bursting through the bathroom door full of husbandly concern, I'm sure. Won't he be surprised to find the door unlocked? And I won't shield my body with my hands—well the frothy bubbles might cover me up just a little bit accidentally, but I can pose with my eyes closed in a glamorous way and it will all be very much like Marilyn Monroe, in . . . in . . . what was that movie called again? I'm distracted because I just watched an ant crawl into my open bottle of bubble bath. It's the kind of bubble bath that's shaped like a pink champagne bottle with gold foil wrapped around the neck. Nathan bought it for me as a welcome home present and it sits next to the can of Raid ant spray on this little ledge. At the time I was really bothered that he got me bubble bath when I don't even take baths. But now I see that doesn't really matter.

Also on the bathtub ledge, sits a little bejeweled picture frame that my mother gave me. It has a quote on it, (of course) "You've come a long way, baby." I look at the picture inside and try not to wince. It's the only photo that I saved from my heavier days. It was buried in the bottom of my underwear drawer and just recently, I bravely inserted it in this frame. I've been waiting for Nathan's shocked commentary or some reaction. Surely one morning he must have glanced this way and choked on his shaving cream.

Nathan has never said a word. At first I wondered if he even realized that the picture was actually of me. But it turns out that before our wedding, during my bachelorette party, my mother had Nathan over for dinner to get to know her future son-in-law better. That evening she diligently walked him through my life via photo albums, narrating my Dolly Parton period, my geeky chapter, my beautician stage, my pregnancy time, my divorce era, my eating disorder days, and finally my obese phase. And in spite of all that, Nathan still married me. Or could it be because of all that?

I lean back in the soapy water and think this is the perfect time to do a breast self-exam. Just like Sam taught me, I glide my fingers evenly over my slick skin and everything is perfectly clear. My breasts are like buoys in the water, completely unsinkable. I remember a time not too long ago, when not only would I have wanted them to sink; I would've drowned them myself. But now I understand that it's good to have something keeping you afloat.

My mother has her quotations to keep her afloat. They also keep her grounded, I realize. And really, there's not a lot wrong with learning from famous people's life experiences and memorizing them as your own. My mother told me two things yesterday that I really liked. I'm thinking of using them as future chapter titles. The first was, "To thyself be true," and the other was, "Show your true colors." Yes, they're a little trite and she probably didn't have to quote both to me in the same day, but perhaps she is reminding herself as well.

My mother has also taken to suggesting that she accompany me on my visits to see my father and yesterday, I let her in on our grand master plan. As we walked in the front entrance of Sunny Creek Village, she helped me fasten my jacket up over my prominent bulge; both of us amused as we realized that my gaining weight had its advantages. Passing by the check-in nurse, I thought I saw her sniff the air but I could have imagined it.

In my dad's room, we laughingly shushed his roommate as we unzipped my jacket and out tumbled a baker's dozen assorted donuts from Winchell's. We fed them to everyone, including little Charlie, who did such a fine job keeping quiet inside my coat. He liked the raspberry filled one the best and clapped his hands in front of my father. My dad took one look at the baby and remarked how exciting it was that we had a foursome for the golf course now. Then he held him on his lap.

When I returned home from my father's place, Nathan had changed the locks on the doors and I got scared that he had changed his mind about us. But he explained that he was thinking about our home "break-in" a while back and wanted to play it safe. He added that this time he wouldn't be giving a key to my mother because he was confident we could handle any emergency, just he and I.

At that point I knew it was time to really talk, so I took a deep breath.

"Nathan, I was the one sending myself those notes back then, using my cell phone to make hang-up calls and typing those anonymous emails," I confessed. "Also, nobody ever chased me when I went jogging." I added that last part for good measure.

"I knew that, Nordis," Nathan had said and hugged me. "You're the only one I know who would stalk herself."

"I was just trying to see if you cared."

"And I was trying to show you that I trusted you implicitly because I knew our marriage was strong and built on a solid foundation. But it was getting hard."

"Oh," I said and hesitated a long time, "And that one night after Karaoke. With Paul?" It was barely a whisper and I waited, holding my breath.

"I didn't want to tell you about that," he hesitated.

No, Nathan, please. I couldn't bear it if you snapped and did something horrific and intentionally violent that night. And all on account of my foolishness.

"My sister had been having an affair. The baby she was carrying wasn't Paul's. She asked me to come over that night after Karaoke for moral support so she could confess and beg his forgiveness. Paul flipped out when he heard and came at Karen with a knife. I had to restrain him with my bare hands and afterwards, I gave him a sedative to calm him down, something I give my patients," Nathan looked down at this point and paused momentarily. "Nobody knew how much Paul had to drink earlier in the evening," he finally continued. "He . . . well he . . . slipped into a lethal coma, apparently during the night. In the morning, Karen typed that note to protect me." Nathan looked directly at me and I looked down at my shoes, which gave Nathan a perfect view of my double chin. It crossed my mind that Sam might be free today if I were as quick thinking as Karen and had written a suicide note.

I still couldn't meet Nathan's eyes and I'm sure he thought it was because I judged him. Nathan continued filling the air with his nervous jabbering.

"The irony is that Paul ranted and raved how he would never raise another man's child. But after finding his lifeless body, Karen lost the baby the next morning." I nodded, remembering that tragic phone call well.

I didn't know what to say to Nathan at that point. I was stunned and began to contemplate. I wanted to tell him how much we had in common but I couldn't risk the confession. Nathan accidentally overdosed his brother-in-law and I accidentally killed my childhood friend. But is that really the way it happened? Ruth's freshly sheared blond hair hung limply in my hand at the salon all those years ago. Large amounts of blood oozed from her blond head on that wood floor just a few months ago. I am so adept at describing things in my writing and convincing even myself. Accidental or intentional? A blur of lines between fiction and reality? In my despair, in my utter despair, I may have pushed that heavy marble sculpture onto Ruth. After all, there was no camera or video to capture the memory. So who knows how it really happened? Did it really happen? Perhaps Nathan's situation wasn't accidental either. Maybe he just put it in terms I could handle. I wondered if Nathan cowered anxiously when he heard sirens in the street like I did? Was this something we'd each carry with us for the rest of our lives? Alone or together?

Just as I was trying to figure out something fitting to add to the conversation, Nathan had grabbed me, kissing me fast and frenetic. Before I could plot out safe positions or change into cover-up lingerie, I felt myself responding to him in a deep, primal way. As we both slid breathlessly down onto the floor, our bodies writhing and thrashing in climactic ecstasy, I remember being grateful for one thing—my mother no longer had a key to the front door.

Afterward, as we lay panting, perspiring and peaceful, I noticed that Nathan had been wearing jeans and a striped tee shirt and not his normal suited attire. What transpired next was more surprising than our spontaneous, uninhibited lovemaking. Nathan told me if I wanted to, we could try again. At first I thought he meant another round of indoor wrestling. Then it hit me and I felt foolish for not getting it right away. Nathan was offering me the opportunity to try again for a daughter! After he swore to me we were finished and that this was it for him. It was so touching of him to bring it up.

"But we do have a daughter," I said simply. When Nathan looked confused, I tried to articulate that our little girl was now the sunshine and the light in my life. She would warm my heart as she danced off the glistening ocean and dazzled with her glow at dusk. I no longer saw that bright, shining ball in the sky as harsh and glaring; hurting my eyes and burning my skin. She shined for all of us, but she especially brightened my days with her constant ray of life sustaining goodness. I gave a little half smile at that last statement because I didn't want to reveal Bridget's middle name. Some things were still nice to keep secret. But Nathan returned my half smile with a full grin of his own. And that's when I first realized—Nathan finally "got" me.

I sigh deeply, thinking back on all this as I see the last of the soap bubbles dissolve. It has been eight full hours of waterlogged thinking. I can't wait much longer for Nathan to come in. In fact I don't think Nathan is coming in at all. Ever. I think Nathan believes he's doing me a kindness, a favor, by giving me my privacy and a little peace and quiet so I can think. And that is his perspective. After all, at the end of the day (I hate it when people say that) all that matters is that we're thinking of each other. How we express it doesn't really matter.

What's this? Someone just slid a thin, white envelope through the crack under the door. I crane my neck and recognize it's a stamped letter. Nathan must've gotten the mail and this one is addressed to me. Another editor's rejection letter for my writing? If I extend my body enough I can just about reach it from the bath. I'm paralyzed as I see the upper left hand corner. It is from Sam. Sam.

The whole letter is quite personal and private so I won't be sharing it here. My philosophy on secrets hasn't changed that much yet. But there is some marvelous news I will share. It seems that Sam's attorney had his charges reduced and he's been given a parole date. A jolt zaps through my entire body when I see it in writing. "November 11, in the year 2011." Or 11-11-11. I can see Sam's smiling eyes as he wrote this magical number.

I look at my white terrycloth robe hanging on the door hook. I will get up and tie it nice and loose around my breasts, so Nathan can sneak a peak later if he wants. I will tousle the twin's hair, tickle Charlie's chin and pretend wrestle with the whole lot of them on the living room carpet. Heck, I might even take them swimming. They are rumble, tumble, roughneck boys and I've learned to adore their energy. Finally, I will smile at my family, a cracked, chapped, raisin-lipped smile from many long hours of being submerged in my fluid thoughts.

Maybe Nathan and I will have another serious talk. About secrets. And about truths.

But before I do anything at all, I first remove my other contact lens, my right one, with a wrinkled finger. Tomorrow morning Nathan is performing laser surgery on my eyes so my vision will be 20/20 again (like hindsight) and soon I will have absolute clarity for our future.

This is it. I release the lens into the water and watch it get wrapped up in a floating strand of my curly, red hair. It pulls, a struggle, snagged by its captor, but suddenly breaks free on its own, where it immediately gets caught in the whirlpool by the drain. I watch it slide down with the last of the bath water—a loud, slurping gurgle. No doubt, it will join my left contact lens. And this is good because things that come in pairs should always stay together.

The End

Made in the USA